SINNERS AND SAINTS

SINNERS AND SAINTS

STORIES OF UPSTATE NEW YORK

BY GEORGE W. WALTER

FAY EDWARD FAULKNER PRINTING COMPANY
SHERBURNE, NEW YORK

ISBN 978-0-932052-31-5

For

FRANCIS AND INEZ LALLY
of Little Falls — my aunt and uncle
whose encouragement and help,
made this book possible

These latest stories by George Walter cover a wider area of Upstate New York than his previous books. While still covering folklore from the Chenango Valley, the book also contains material from the Herkimer - Ilion area.

As with his other books, Mr. Walter drew from many sources; scrapbooks, newspaper clippings, books, and of course his tape recordings with friends and relatives in the area where the stories occur.

A glance at the Table of Contents page will show the reader the diversity with which the many stories relate. The early days of Upstate New York were exciting times. Strong and weak, red and white, "Sinner or Saint," these people are a part of our heritage.

This will probably be the last publication in book form of Mr. Walters' work. It is with sadness that we report Mr. Walters passing during the early days of publishing this book.

The Publishers

TABLE OF CONTENTS

THE INDIAN'S BELL

There are four historic buildings within a twenty-mile stretch on Route 5S on the south side of the Mohawk River in Herkimer County. They are in this order, the Spinner House in Mohawk; the Fort Herkimer Church, General Herkimer's homestead and the Indian Castle Church.

I was six years old that Sunday morning when I first heard the bell of the old Indian Castle Church. Accompanied by my pretty, golden-haired Aunt Inez, who was only a few years older than myself, we had come by train from her home in Little Falls, on what was the first lap of our journey to the old Walter homestead in the hamlet of Newville.

The dusty roads near the small railroad station were alive with people. While many were walking, others were driving along in carriages and democrat wagons.

"Look," I said pointing, "all the people seem glad to hear the bell."

"They are happy to hear it ring," my aunt answered, "for it was some of their ancestors who saved it from the Indians many long years ago."

As we followed the winding road on foot through the gorges, to Newville, I heard for the first time, the story of the Indian Castle Church bell.

The church was built in 1769 by Sir William Johnson on a bluff overlooking Nowadaga Creek, for his Mohawks. The church marks the site of the upper castle inhabited by the Bear Clan of the Mohawks between 1700-1775.

The church cost Sir William $142.75 to build. Samuel Clyde was in charge and John David Muller was the carpenter. It required 276 days of work, according to Sir. William's papers. The boss carpenter received seven shillings a day for his services while Sovia Parr, the cook received one shilling. The lumber came from George Klock and Ebenezer Cox. Provisions came from Johannes Nellis store at Fort Nellis, one mile east of St. Johnsville. Adam Thurn was the blacksmith. The helpers were Dygert, Herkimer, Zimmerman, Fox, Dillenbeck, Syfert (Seeber) and Walrath.

The wooden building was painted to represent stone. It was thirty two feet by fifty feet in size. The steeple had a large weathercock, surmounted by a gilded ball. The only door was on the side. The church was equipped with an hour glass pulpit and sounding board.

The Rev. Harry Monro of St. Peter's Episcopal Church at Albany conducted the first service on June 17, 1770. At that time Sir William Johnson presented the building to the Mohawks.

The gift was received by Joseph Brant, who had donated the land.

The bell in the steeple tolled almost endlessly on those Sunday mornings to please the Indians. It had been cast in England and the Indians never tired of listening to its velvet tones.

When the day came that the fighting valley militia drove the tories and Indians to Canada, the church was taken over by white settlers as a house of worship.

Then one night the Mohawks returned and stole their beloved treasure from the belfry of the church and sank it in the river and later floated it down to the "marked tree".

For many days thereafter the German Paltinate settlers searched vainly for the bell, but were unable to unearth any clues as to its whereabouts. Finally giving up in dispair, they settled back to wait the time the Mohawks would return to remove the bell from its hiding place.

Time passed. Then one dark night the Indians again stealthy invaded the settlement. They may have been a little over confident. The bell was raised carefully from the river bed and suspended on a long pole. As it was covered with mud and slime from its immersion, some of the Mohawks became doubtful whether it would ever again toll as it had in the past.

Disregarding the consequences, one savage loosened the clapper and the bell pealed loudly. The Indians rejoiced at the sound and the bell sent out its appealing call throughout the settlement.

Soon from every home the settlers rushed with their muskets primed. The Indians dropped their precious bell and fled.

The settlers restored the bell to the church belfry. It was dented and there was a small crack in its side where it had struck a stone when the Indians abandoned it.

"The people listen on Sunday morning for the bell," Aunt Inez explained, "just as their people did before them. Like their ancestors, they are happy to know their bell is safe."

LOVER'S LEAP

Along the northern edge of the city limits of Little Falls, Herkimer County, where the cliffs rise upward a hundred feet, there was a promontory widely known in Mohawk Valley history as "Lover's Leap."

Long before the New York Central Railroad cut along the face of the cliffs for its roadbed, a circular cavity, with an opening about ten feet across, facing the turbulent river, was near the top of the cliff. A massive lintel hung over the entrance of this cavity, whcih might have been planted by humans. Within the cave light filtered through an opening in the rocks overhead. I was told years ago that an Indian brave and the woman he loved once lived there and jumped into the river so they might be together always.

According to legend it was at the cliff top that the feud between two young Mohawk chiefs reached its climax. One of the chiefs was of the Wolf Clan, the other of the Tortoise Clan. The maiden they loved was of the Bear Clan.

For many moons the young chiefs wooed the daughter of the old chief of the Bear Clan. He made each man believe he was the most favored. In battle against the Mingoes and the Mohegans the two young chiefs had fought beside the old chief, and he was well aware of their bravery and eligibility.

The young maiden was in love with the chief of the Wolf Clan and consented to be his woman. The chief of the Tortoise Clan flew into a jealous rage when he learned of the maiden's decision. Swearing revenge, he decided to possess the maid before the Wolf chief could take her into his home. He cloaked his emotions under a mask of friendliness as he congratulated his rival, and swore long and devoted friendship.

Carefully awaiting an opportunity to carry out his plans, the Tortoise continued his deception until the Wolf departed up the river on a hunting trip leaving the maiden in his protection.

Unsuspecting the danger that loomed nearby, the girl often walked with the Tortoise in the moonlight. As time passed and the bridal day drew nearer, the Tortoise decided to strike. While walking with the girl along the river's edge one night, he casually proposed a journey to the little island in the river where the fireflies sparkled. As the Tortoise's canoe was near, the girl agreed. After the Tortoise shoved his canoe out into the river, he ignored the island and swung his frail craft into the swift current and skillfully made for the northern shore where the cliffs rose high into the sky.

As the canoe touched the opposite bank, the Tortoise leaped ashore and pulled the craft up partly out of the water, tying it to a tree with a narrow length of green deer hide. Frightened, and realizing the intentions of her supposed friend, the maiden leaped from the canoe and started to run swiftly along the shore line. With incredible speed, the Tortoise leaped after her and caught her in his arms. As she cried for help and struggled to escape, the chief silenced her with a blow and clapped a hand over her mouth. Still fighting, the Tortoise carried her up the side of the cliff to the cave where he dumped her on a pile of soft skins inside.

It was a great moment of triumph for the Tortoise who had planned well. Having long known of the cavern, he had stocked it with provisions and bedding.

While returning from hunting the following day, the Wolf saw the Tortoise's canoe on the shore below the mouth of the cave. Thinking nothing of the matter, he continued homeward down the river anxious to see his betrothed. Upon his arrival at the camp, the girl's father greeted him with the news that his daughter and the Tortoise had fled the previous night. Remembering his supposed friend's canoe on the opposite shore and suspecting what had happened, the Wolf sat down to patiently await the coming of the night.

When the moon was again high overhead, the Wolf silently embarked in his canoe. Skillfully he swung into the swift current and paddled for the northern shore. Landing near the spot where the Tortoise's canoe was tied, the Wolf lifted his canoe from the river and secreted it in some bushes nearby. After loosening the knife and tomahawk in his belt he started up the steep cliff towards the cavern.

The light of the full moon revealed the interior of the cave. Directly below him lay the Tortoise with his unwilling sweetheart in his arms. The sight blinded the Wolf with anger. Taking his tomahawk from its sheath, he leaped lightly into the chamber and swung a murderous blow at the Tortoise's head. It would have cleaved his skull if it had struck him squarely, but in the dim light, the Wolf miscalculated, the weapon glanced and struck the rocky wall. The Tortoise awoke with a mingled cry of pain and fear. He leaped to his feet and fled through the cavern's entrance. The Wolf started to follow; He tripped over the maiden on the floor. As he regained his footing, a huge boulder crashed down blocking the entrance of the cavern. The Wolf pulled the girl to her feet. Tearfully she told of her abduction.

Realizing that the Tortoise would soon return with his warriors to kill them, the Wolf tried to force the boulder from the entrance. Unable to move the boulder, the Wolf began groping towards the fissures above his head where the moonlight streamed through. He lifted the maiden in his arms and she quickly climbed through the largest opening. Reaching for a strong branch of a tree she pushed it down through the fissure to the bottom of the cave. The Wolf climbed out.

In the distance they could hear the yelling of the Tortoise and his warriors as they paddled their canoes towards them. Clinging to the precipitous trail, the Wolf and his sweetheart descended to the shore, within a few lengths of their enemies. The Wolf retrieved his canoe from the hiding place and launched it in the river. Quickly climbing into it, the Wolf bade the maiden to be still while he abruptly turned the frail craft straight for the cataracts. The canoe swept away from the pursuers into the boiling waters and passed unharmed into the placid waters of the gulf below.

Down the broad Mohawk River the Wolf and his maid sped into the distance. Upon the margin of a lower lake they made their home and lived for two generations, seeing their children hunt and go forth to battle.

In the long line of their descent, it is said, came Joseph Brant, the great Mohawk sachem, the strong Wolf of his nation.

THE IRON HOUSE

Hannibal Hamlin Cady was such a strong believer in the Bible's prediction that the world would be destroyed by fire, he built an iron house on Mutton Hill as a protection. The house, actually a small one story shack, outlasted the builder.

Cady came to Madison County early in the 1890's with his parents, Mr. and Mrs. Seneca Cady and older brother, Solon Cato Cady. It was reported the family came from North Carolina, fleeing a step ahead of the moonshiners.

"The Cady family was so deeply religious and of such conscientious nature they told the revenuers where some moonshiners had their still," John Clair Battey of Oneida, who was well acquainted with the family recalled. "The revenuers went into the hills and destroyed the stills.

"The next morning a facsimile of a coffin was found on the Cady doorstep with the words '24 hours' written on it. The family picked up their clothes and left. I do not think any of them ever went back."

Battey said several years later he found a letter from a cousin of Hannibal Cady's on the floor of his iron house. "It was dated 1896-07," he said, "and the writer said she had a chance to sell the home, as there were tourists coming who might be interested. It was evident the family had paid the taxes on their southern property and kept title to it."

When they came to Madison County the family settled across the road, near the district school in Pleasant Valley, some two miles north of Buck's Woods. The house, which is still standing, had a white picket fence around the dooryard.

Seneca Cady is remembered as being of average height and rather bony. "Being such a strict vegetarian, it didn't give him any chance of putting on any fat," Battey remarked.

"Cady had his front yard so full of burdocks, a dog couldn't get through them," Battey said. "He liked the deep purple flowers on them."

"I was just a kid going to the Pleasant Valley School in those days," the Oneidan continued, "I was the youngest of my family who attended. Hannibal Cady seemed to like us kids and was always glad to see us when we came over to his

17

home at noon. The Cady's had a 24-pipe organ in their home and Cady used to play on it for us. Other times he would take us out into the barn.

"Although the family kept a few chickens and raised a few sheep they never killed or ate them or the eggs. Cady had a straw cutter in the barn, and we kids thought it was fun to operate it by cranking the cutter.

"Hannibal seemed to take delight if he could keep us so busy we were late for school," Battey said. "It seemed to be the height of his ambition to try and keep us at his home until after one o'clock."

Hannibal had gone to Poughkeepsie Business College years before, but there is no evidence of his having utilized his education.

"A fellow who roomed with him said Hannibal lived on peanuts and carrots," Battey remembered. "The two youths were supposed to share the joint expenses of the room and food. Hannibal's roommate was unable to live in such a manner, and quit."

Hannibal did go up to my father and mother's (Mr. and Mrs. Clarence Battey) home," Battey said. "He ate popcorn that had been popped in grease and had salt on it, and did not seem to mind."

The Cady family was guided by the Bible, but never attended any church. They were extremely religious.

Battey was unable to recall when the Cady's moved to Mutton Hill. Located in the Town of Fenner, Mutton Hill is one of the highest points in Madison County. It received its name from the sheep old Peter Smith of Peterboro, who owned nearly a million acres, used to pasture there. The road leads from Nelson to Cazenovia.

Mr. and Mrs. Cady and their son, Hannibal bought a farm on the western side of the road, in the midst of a small grove of maple trees.

"Hannibal and my father, Clarence Battey were very good friends," Battey said, "and they used to go fox hunting together.

"Father walked over to the Cady home one day. Hannibal showed father his bed. It was inside a piano box.

"When I get in there I close the door," Hannibal said, "anybody that comes in would never think of looking for me in the piano box," Battey recalled.

"At that time I think old Seneca Cady was dead. I remember it was in the middle of the winter when Hannibal drove down to Cazenovia and went to the undertakers, and said, 'When you get around to it, I wish you'd come up and bury my mother.'

" 'Why? When did she die?' the undertaker asked.

" 'Well, I don't know,' Cady replied, 'four or five days ago, I guess.'

" 'I think I'd better go right up,' the undertaker said. Later he told acquaintances that he found Mrs. Cady frozen as stiff as a mackerel.

"I remember seeing Hannibal during the middle of one winter in Cazenovia," Battey said. "He was quite a big man with sandy hair and long, red whiskers. He usually wore a long fur coat and a straw hat winter and summer. When I saw him he had a team of horses hitched to a two wheel 'thing-a-ma-jig.' It consisted of the two hind wheels and axle off a farm wagon, on which he had fitted a high box and a pole. He put a platform on top of the box with railings around it, so that the sides of his cart were just about the height of his head. He drove this to town all of the time."

Solon Cady returned home only once, Battey believes. He stayed overnight and then left.

"He told acquaintances in Peterboro, 'My God, I can't stand the way they are living. Maybe it was all right when I was a kid but, I have got over that way now,' " Battey said.

Solon may have brought some gold samples back with him, and probably stirred his brother's interest in geology.

Roy W. Cary of the Mile-Strip recalled Hannibal often showed his gold samples to the children and talked about mining. A former rural delivery mail carrier remembered that Hannibal received more magazines than anyone else on his route.

Hannibal Cady read and reread his Bible many times and his belief in it never wavered. However, the prediction concerning the destruction of the earth by fire worried him. He began to build his iron house on the east side of the road.

"This house won't burn up," he told friends, "but the rest of them will."

The framework of his "house" was of two by four's. It was one room with a few boards laid over the top for storage. He sheathed it with large strips of iron, excepting for the small, four-paned windows on each side. The interior was never finished. A small stove furnished the heat. A well house about 50 feet in front of the house furnished him water and a place to keep his vegetables. A small barn stood behind the house in which he kept his team.

No one ever remembers Cady working his land, but he must have cut some hay or weeds to feed the horses.

He lived on vegetables, herbs, nuts and raisins. Cady always paid his taxes. No one is able to definitely say what happened to his parents' home and farm. The house is no longer standing.

Cady continued to live in solitary bachelorhood until he was old and gray. He was bothered by rheumatism and had difficulty in getting about, and was unable to hitch or drive his team. Friends and neighbors often brought him wood for his stove and vegetables to eat.

During the 1920's Cady was practically helpless. Cary, who was also a former Town of Fenner welfare officer, recalled one particularly severe winter the old man was found by a neighbor on the frozen earth of his wellhouse where he had crawled. The State Police were called, and in turn, Cary was notified.

"Cady had an aversion to going to the County Home at Eaton," the former welfare officer said. "He was a pretty independent old man. We couldn't leave him to freeze in his unheated iron shack.

"I told him that going to the County Home was nothing to be ashamed of, as he had paid his taxes for years," Cary related. "I finally talked him into going."

"At the County Home the attendants gave him what probably was his first bath in years. Then they dressed him in some good clothing and placed him in a wheel chair.

"I remember that first night they had hamburger to eat at the home, Cary said. "Old Cady had never eaten meat before in his life, but he ate some and liked it.

"He had never seen or heard a radio before. From the time someone tuned it in, Cady was the first to listen and the last one to go to bed," Cary added.

Although Commissioner of Public Welfare William Liddle of Hamilton searched the records in the Madison County Courthouse in Wampsville, he was unable to find any mention of Cady's admittance to the county home or account of his death.

Battey said the last time he saw Hannibal Cady alive was in 1930 or '31.

"I worked for an Oneida oil company and used to deliver fuel oil over to the county home," he said. "One day I asked Herman McIntyre, the county superintendent, if Cady was living there. 'Yes, he's here,' Mr. McIntyre replied.

"I went in to see him. I found him sitting in a wheel chair. I told him who I was, but I had the impression he never realized I was there. Cady must have been about eighty years of age at that time."

Cary said when Cady died, he had left a stipulation that no funeral service be held for him and that his grave be left without a marker. His wishes were carried out.

WITCHES IN THE VALLEY

A gentle family horse that suddenly became unmanageable; cream that failed to churn into butter and bleating sheep when there were none in the area .... These are some of the stories of witchcraft told in the lower Mohawk Valley.

Witchcraft has always been partly hidden in the background of the descendants of the German Palatinate settlers. The elderly residents still speak of "witchin's", but claim it is no longer practiced.

Great, great Aunt Matilda Bauder who resided in the vicinity of Glen, was reported to have been a witch. Residents claim she cast a spell on a black horse owned by Mrs. Louis Van Avery. In the morning when Mrs. Van Avery went to the barn to harness her horse, she would find his mane and tail braided. It did not matter how many times Mrs. Van Avery unbraided them, the next morning they would be braided tighter than ever.

The horse, which was ordinarily docile, became so vicious, no one could drive him. Mrs. Van Avery was told if she had the tail docked and the mane clipped, it would break the spell. She soon had this done and the horse became docile again. Mrs. Van Avery had no further trouble from Aunt Matilda.

In order to learn more about the antics of the witches, I drove to Randall in the summer of 1941 and spent some time with Mr. and Mrs. William Leonardson, relatives of my family, I found Aunt Matilda Bauder was a great aunt of my grandmother, Mrs. Anna Bennet, who once resided in Glen.

"There used to be a family named Craig who resided in Randall several years ago," Mr. Leonardson said. "When Mr. Craig went to the barn in the morning to milk the cows, he found no sign of them. In their place there was the exact number of turkeys roosting on the stanchions.

"Mr. Craig rushed back into the house and told his wife their cows were missing and in their place were turkeys.

"Go on out again," his wife instructed. "The cows are all right."

"Mr. Craig returned to the barn and as his wife said, the cows were in their stanchions," Mr. Leonardson said. "There wasn't a turkey in sight."

"If Mr. Craig went out at night to visit a neighbor, as soon as he left his home, he would find a small dog chasing after him, nibbling at his heels. The dog would keep pestering him until he was safe in his own home again." Mr. Leonardson said. "Then the dog would disappear."

"Mrs. Leonardson leaned forward in her rocking chair as soon as her husband had finished.

"After Will and I were married, we used to live on the old Applegate farm," she recalled. "Will liked to sit in the doorway playing his violin. He would often see lights out by the well at night."

"That is true," Mr. Leonardson said. "I'd call her, but she would never see anything. "You know it isn't everybody who can see those things."

"Mrs. Applegate was said to be a witch," Mrs. Leonardson said. "There was a couple who resided near her who began to see lights dancing about the farm at night. When they went out and looked around, the witch lights would go bobbing along the stone fences. If they approached them, the lights would vanish.

"Sometimes the couple would see hogs on their straw-stack and hear sheep bleating. "The man and his wife were really frightened," Mrs. Leonardson said, "because they had no hogs or sheep on their farm. In the morning they would go out and find no signs of the animals anywhere.

"When the woman tried to churn her cream, she found she was unable to get butter or buttermilk," Mrs. Leonardson continued. "This made the couple certain it was a witch who was plaguing them. They finally consulted a witch doctor.

"This was a male witch doctor," Mrs. Leonardson said. "He told the woman to heat a new horseshoe red hot, then spit on it and drop it into her churn with the cream the next time.

" 'The cream will make butter and you will get buttermilk,' the witch doctor said, adding, 'Let me warn you to get the butter and buttermilk out of the way and do not allow anyone to have any. Clear out of the house yourself and don't come back until the next day.'

"The couple did exactly as the witch doctor told them," Mrs. Leonardson said. "The woman had no trouble with her churning. When she finished she put the butter and buttermilk in the pantry. The couple then went to a neighbors to spend the night.

23

"When they returned they discovered some of the butter and buttermilk had been taken from the pantry. They went to the witch doctor and told what had happened," Mrs. Leonardson said. "The doctor told the couple he had just come from Mrs. Applegates. The old lady's throat was burned and she was burned all through her. She died in great agony.

" 'She was the witch,' the doctor said. 'When she ate your butter and drank your buttermilk the heat from the horseshoe burned through her. If you had given her any of your churning she would have come back on you. The horseshoe would not have affected her," the doctor said.

"My father married my mother in 1854," Mrs. Leonardson said, "they went to live in a house that stood between this house and the Erie Canal. The house was haunted.

"Often while my father and mother were in their parlor sitting, they would hear noises in their cellar, such as if someone was tipping over their cider and apple barrels. When Pa went down cellar, he would find nothing disturbed."

At other times, Mrs. Leonardson said her parents would hear the stacked firewood in the woodshed slipping and crashing to the floor. When the woodshed was inspected, everything was in order.

"Pa was an early riser," Mrs. Leonardson said. "One morning after he left for work, my mother was suddenly surprised to awaken to find a strange man standing beside her bed. Mother was frightened almost out of her wits.

" 'In the name of God, what do you want?' she cried.

" 'Don't be afraid,' the man said. 'Do you know where there is a Negro family living?'

"Yes," Mother told him, "There are a couple of Negro families living between here and Fultonville."

"Thank you," the stranger said gently. He lifted one of Mother's hands from the coverlit and kissed it. Releasing her hand, the stranger left.

"My parents never were able to find out why the stranger was seeking a Negro family," Mrs. Leonardson remarked. "From that day on there were no further disturbances in my parents home."

THE LAST SURVIVOR

He was a man of mystery. His exact birthplace is unknown; he was an army veteran, but his name does not appear on the service rolls. Because he used an assumed name, it required a special act of Congress to grant him a pension.

His real name was Daniel Frederick Bachman, but he took the name of Bakeman. He was the last surviving pensioned veteran of the Revolutionary War. When he died at the age of one hundred and nine years, it was recalled he had cast his first vote for General George Washington and his last for General Ulysses S. Grant for the presidency.

Bachman or Bakeman, as he was known in his later years, was married to the same woman for eighty-one years. Today, his descendants spread across New York, Pennsylvania and Nebraska.

Bachman was born September 28, 1759, but his birthplace is a subject of conjecture. Some believe he was a Dutchman, born in New Jersey. Others who knew his children believe he was born on Firey Hill, near Newville, in Herkimer County or in the VanHornsville-Starkville area. He married Susan Brewer in 1782. She is also believed to have been born in the Newville area. Like their descendants, the Monks, Walter and Bettingers, Bachman is believed to be of Palatinate German descent.

The index of the Daughters of the American Revolution, lists him under the name of Bakeman. The index also lists a John Bachman, who was born in 1731 and died in 1800, and his wife, Christina Smart. There is a possibility they might be Bachman's parents.

When he was young, Bachman lived for many years in the Town of Stark and in the Town of Danube. He was seventeen when the spark of the Revolution ignited. When Chief Joseph Brant and his Mohawks and Captain Walter Butler, his rangers and tories began their raids on the Valley, Bachman became a militiaman.

Although his name does not appear in "The New York Line", a record book of soldiers of the Revolutionary War, family records indicate he served under Lieutenant Colonel Ebenezer Cox of the First Tryon County Regiment, in Captain

Van Arnum's Company. One source claims Bachman fought in the battle of Fort Plain.

Bachman was a farmer. Like most farmers of his time, he also did carpentry work and blacksmithing.

When he changed his name to Bakeman is not known. There is a possibility some town official might have listed it that way. Various histories also have listed him as "Beekman" and "Beakman."

Mr. and Mrs. Bakeman had eight children, Philip, Richard, Christopher, Betsey, Margaret, Susan, Mary and Christine.

In appearance Bakeman was tall, very slender and erect, with a heavy head of hair he managed to keep all his life, and wore chin whiskers.

Three of his homes and their contents were destroyed by fire while he resided in Herkimer County. One home was burned while he was in Albany with a load of potash to sell.

Several of his children married while he and his wife resided in the valley. His daughter, Mary, became the second wife of John Monk, who also was a Revolutionary War veteran. Bakeman's daughter, Margaret, who never married, resided with the William Walter family of Newville. Walter was married to Mary Monk. Mr. and Mrs. Bakeman visited the Walter home on Firey Hill many times.

When Mrs. Susan Bakeman was visiting at the Stephen Maxwell home in Stark , she fell and broke her leg. It was set and healed.

In 1825, Mr. and Mrs. Bakeman joined the westward movement. He was 66 and his wife, 67, when they packed their belongings in a wagon and started westward. Their son, Christopher, accompanied them.

The family settled in Arcade, a hamlet then in the Town of China in Genesee County. Arcade was a post village in the southern part of the town, forty miles southwest of Batavia. It had a Presbyterian Church, a grist mill, several sawmills, a carding and cloth dressing mill; two stores, a temperance tavern and about fifty dwellings. Bakeman built his home on the north side of the County Road.

When Wyoming County was formed from the southern part of Genesee County in 1841, the Town of China and hamlet of Arcade became a part of the new county.

Four years later, Mr. and Mrs. Bakeman moved to the Town of Freedom in Cattaraugus County where they were to live out their lives. The population of the town was about 1,831.

Bakeman was described by William Vernon Smith, a Michigan attorney, who knew him well, as "a man of wit and spirit, a jollier and a lover of life. Bakeman never grew too old to enjoy a joke."

"Some men were digging a well and the old man was down maybe sixteen or eighteen feet," Smith recalled. "The bell rang for dinner and the gang went off and left Bakeman down in the well. They hadn't much more than sat down when in he walked. They never got a word out of him as how he climbed out of the well. He left them guessing."

The Wyoming County Mirror, in a July, 1859 issue reported: "At Arcade during the 4th of July observance. Mr. W. H. Wilson introduced Daniel Bakeman and wife, respectively 100 and 102 years old, both having lived before the Revolution and seen every fourth of July celebrated so far."

A few day prior to the observance, Mrs. Bakeman exhibited specimens of her needlework, which she had made without the aid of glasses.

Bakeman was thoroughly filled with the Spirit of '76. Early on the morning of the fourth of July, he would load his old flint lock musket he had carried in the war, and start firing it into the air. He would load the musket and fire it thirteen times in memory of the original thirteen colonies while yelling at the top of his voice, "Hurrah for Washington, Gates, Putnam and Lee and all der brave men who fought for libertee!'"

The old man had no use for those who were friendly with the British.

"I shall never forget one thing," Smith said. "He came to the post office one summer evening and sat down on a dry goods box, about the time the people had got away from work. You know how the country people used to gather around the center and swap lies.

"Well, here was the old man," the attorney said, "and here was Dariah Strong and his brother, William, who had the farm between us and town. Everybody knew that Catherine Herkimer, their mother, was a niece of old General Herkimer. They prided themselves that they were somebody because of this relationship. They came from the same place that Bakeman did.

"Well, Dariah asked Bakeman some questions and I remember the old man didn't warm up to him at all. I didn't know until fifty years later that most of General Herkimer's family went out and made peace with the British after General St. Leger landed on the shore of Lake Ontario and was preparing to march up the Mohawk Valley and join Burgoyne," Smith said.

Bakeman never cared for some members of the Schuyler family who resided near Newville in the Town of Danube, where he previously lived. Peter Schuyler was married to Barbara Herkimer another sister of General Herkimer. One of their sons was Hon Yost Schuyler, whom the old man always considered a traitor and scoundrel.

"Of course, Bakeman was a big figure in our little world", Smith recalled. "He had always been a pioneer farmer, never earning much, never doing anything extraordinary."

As Bakeman had entered the militia when he was about seventeen years of age and served during the last four years of the war, some of his neighbors thought he should receive a pension. With the assistance of his many friends, Bakeman applied for a pension in 1867.

The document reads as follows: "Daniel Frederick Bakeman, the last pensioner of the war of the Revolution, was pensioned at the rate of $500 per annum on Certificate No. 33,429, which was issued July 17, 1867, under a Special Act of Congress, dated February 22, 1867, the bill being reported by Mr. Price of the committee on Revolutionary Pensions. His formal application of pension under said act, was executed before Hyder Barnes, justice of the peace in Arcade, June 17, 1867, in which he stated that he was 107 years old, a resident of Freedom, Cattaraugus County, New York, and that he served during the last four years of the war under Captain Van Arnum and Colonel Willett in the New York Troops."

The delay of nearly fifty years after the act of authorizing the pensioning of Revolutionary soldiers, before this patriot was rewarded was undoubtedly due to the fact of the misspelling of his family name, it having been written Bachman, also Bakeman, Bateman and even Baker."

The $500 pension allowed Bakeman to buy his own horse and carriage. At the annual fourth of July celebrations, the authorities of many communities begged him to participate.

After eighty-one years of married life, Mrs. Bakeman died September 10, 1863, at the age of 105 years.

Bakeman had two nephews residing in the township, Austin and Jacob Bakeman. The old veteran used to go to Jacob's place to visit. It was there that Attorney Smith met Bakeman.

The old Revolutionary War soldier died at the age of one hundred and nine years on April 5, 1869. Both he and his wife are buried in Freedom.

On July 17, 1915, the one hundred and fortieth anniversary of the Battle of Bunker Hill, the Olean Chapter of the Daughters of the American Revolution, marked the graves of Daniel and Susan Bakeman. Members of the chapter presented an American flag, which has become known as the "Bakeman flag" to the Baptist Church, following a parade and all-day observance.

Since then, the graves have been a focal point in Freedom. On fourth of July observances, tribute is paid to Daniel Frederick Bakeman, the last surviving pensioner of the Revolutionary War.

THE PIGEONS FLY NO MORE

There is not a single passenger pigeon left on earth, but it has been less than one hundred years since the last huge flock darkened the skies of Upstate New York.

Early residents have left vivid accounts of the flocks of pigeons, so numerous when they flew over, they darkened the sky and required four or five hours to pass.

G. Frank Barden, a blacksmith at Taberg, related to Mrs. Florence McElroy Simon in 1930, when the flight of 1881 was on, "We had to light lamps. It was twilight and all the time the whirring sound overhead seemed like a great wind that sailed on and on.

"The sky, the air, seemed literally filled with pigeons. Other years, spring and fall, they had passed overhead in great flocks," Barden recalled. "Their passing each time was like a day set apart on the almanac. One said of such and such a happening 'that was a week before the pigeons went over' or 'that was only a day before the pigeons passed.' "

"The last flight was the greatest of all," he said, "it seemed that all the pigeons in the world went over our heads that day. And the next year, not a pigeon."

The blacksmith said he never saw another passenger pigeon.

"It is my belief some calamity struck them, a storm or a disease which simply wiped them out while they were flying on to their winter feeding grounds.

"It does not stand to reason they were slaughtered, those thousands that went over Oneida County," Barden remarked.

The greedy habits of the settlers as well as the Indians in killing the birds made them vanish forever.

"Year after year, we had shot them, trapped them," the blacksmith said. "Barrels full of the pigeons were shipped day after day to New York City and each year there seemed to be no lessening in their number when they came back again in the spring."

The pigeons had their nesting place in the Osceola area. In the spring the birds gathered, breaking the limbs from the trees under their sheer weight. Many of them flew to feeding places 100 miles away after devastating the Osceola countryside.

Indians from the Oneida Reservation moved in for the kill. The braves and squaws with their little babies strapped to their backs, clubbed the birds and even cut down the trees in order to reach the nests and the young. In four to five days the Indians had barrels salted down to sell.

"As for regular trappers, we fellows trapped them by the hundreds" the blacksmith said. "Once, Nort Taft, who followed the birds from nesting place to nesting place throughout the country, trapping them for a business, and I caught 1,200 at one time.

"That was too many for our net. The birds tore it to shreds in their mad fluttering to be free."

"Pigeons, millions of them, darkened the sun, like an eclipse," Barden remembered, "flying on and on with the noise of humming airplanes into the west."

"This one year," he added, "The next year not even one little solitary pigeon flying over to cast its shadow on the green fields. It is a thing to think about."

Mrs. Simon added a footnote to her interview with the blacksmith. She said Mr. Barden was probably the only person in Oneida County who "sleeps on a bed made from the feathers of passenger pigeons."

THE BATTLE OF SHELL'S BUSH

The settlers of Shell's Bush, near Little Falls, were keeping an eye out for the Tories and Indians that August, 1781, as they worked to get their harvests in.

When they learned that a band of Mohawks and Tories under the command of Captain Donald McDonald was on its way, the residents, excepting Mr. and Mrs. Christian Shell and sons, fled to the safety of Fort Dayton at Herkimer. The Shell's had built a strong blockhouse, two stories in height, with no windows on the lower floor. Loopholes were on all sides of the cabin, so those who might be besieged could fire at the enemy from all directions. Shell kept a goodly supply of water, food and ammunition in his blockhouse home for any emergency that might arise. McDonald's force came and captured two of the Shell boys, but the parents and four other sons gained their blockhouse and placed the bar down, blocking the door.

The Tories and Indians immediately attacked the blockhouse from all sides. Shell and his sons poured a deadly fire through the loopholes, while Mrs. Shell kept loading the rifles with ball and shot. Several of the Mohawks lighted arrows that were dipped in resin and shot them at the walls and roof of the blockhouse to set it on fire. However, the logs failed to catch.

Captain McDonald boldly ran up to the door, and attempted to force it open with a crowbar. Shell quickly brought him down with a well-placed shot, wounding him.

The farmer quickly opened the door and dragged the Tory inside and again barred the door. McDonald had some ammunition on his person which the Shell's found useful.

The fall of their leader did not stop the Tories and Mohawks. They were infuriated that they were unable to take the blockhouse. When they ceased their attack for a while Shell believed they had given up. He went into the second story, singing loudly one of his favorite hymns, "A Firm Fortress Is Our Lord."

The enemy had not quit. They suddenly attacked in strength. Five of the Indians managed to thrust the muzzles of their rifles through the loopholes, and while they sighted, it was a critical moment for the defenders who were busy firing from the other loopholes. Snatching an ax, Mrs. Shell struck firm blows on the Mohawks' rifles, bending the muzzles, so they exploded when the Indians pulled the triggers.

The withering fire from the blockhouse caused the attackers to withdraw. Darkness was coming on, and the family knew the Indians and Tories would try to gain entrance as soon as it got dark.

Shell decided to try a little strategy. Going to the second floor, he called loudly to his wife, that a relief party was on its way from Fort Dayton. A few minutes later as the darkness deepened, he shouted, "Captain Small, march your company around the side of the house."

"Captain Getmen, you had better bring your men up on the left side," the farmer yelled.

As Mr. and Mrs. Shell had prayed, he was able to fool the enemy into thinking that a large party of troops were upon them. The Tories and Indians turned and fled.

The family's markmanship had killed 11 of the attackers and wounded six others. Not one of the defenders was wounded.

The Shell's remained in their cabin all night, expecting the enemy to return, but they failed to. The next day they removed their wounded prisoner to Fort Dayton. However, Captain McDonald died after an operation.

Christian Shell and two of his sons were working in the field near the blockhouse home shortly afterwards. Some of the Mohawks who had concealed themselves in the wheat field, suddenly opened fire. One of the boys was killed, the father wounded, but another son who was helping them, escaped. Shell was removed to Fort Dayton, but never recovered from his wound.

The two sons who were carried away by the Indians and Tories during McDonald's raid, were taken to Canada, but their lives were spared. After the war they were freed and returned home.

Today the site of the battle of the Shell family is commemorated by a Daughter of the American Revolution marker.

THE ROBBERY OF COL. THOMPSON

Colonel Erastus Thompson, whose title was given him for his work in the militia, seemed to hate practically everyone and everything. A boss carpenter and later a farmer, he was extremely cruel to his family and to his horses and cows.

Colonel Thompson was long remembered in the Earlville-Lebanon area for his uncontrollable temper. When he and his family were robbed of $1,220 on Tuesday night, August 3, 1875, he received little sympathy.

John Parsons of Earlville remembered that during the winter of 1854, the colonel worked hard making doors, window frames, inside trim and shaping the flooring. The basswood and butternut lumber had been cut on the Parsons' farm.

Parsons liked to recall Thompson's temper tantrums.

"When he had worked hours on one door, he discovered an error that would not let it go together," Parsons said, "so he took his hand ax and smashed it all to pieces. Afterward he handed father the pay for the nice butternut lumber he spoiled.

"On another occasion when shingling a barn he pounded his thumb," Parsons continued. "He threw the hammer as far as possible into two-foot high grass, then spent an hour finding it."

The Parsons' new home was built in 1855. For his work as boss carpenter, he received the salary of $1.25 per day with board.

As Colonel Thompson grew older and more vitriolic in nature, residents of the area would not hire him to do any work. He eventually bought a farm of over 100 acres just "over the hill" west of Earlville. Parsons said it was the farm owned by John Conley in 1942.

The old colonel kept about 20 cows. He never fed them any grain, believing it was a waste of time and money. In warm weather they ate the sparse grass in the pasture, and in the winter lived on hay. The small amount of milk the cows gave went to the Cold Spring Cheese Factory, down the valley, about half a mile from his farm.

Thompson owned one horse, and was as cruel to the animal as he was his cows. He did all his farm work with the one horse, and even had a one-horse mowing machine.

The old man was equally as hard on his family. He never drank hard cider or liquor as many of the area residents did, and never took any recreation. He made his wife do the washing, ironing, cooking and baking, as well as help with the farm work.

The colonel made his two daughters, Celia and Kate work as hard as their mother. As soon as they reached young womanhood, both left home. His son, Frank Thompson, did a man's work when he was a mere child. He was undernourished and undersized, and had little formal education. Neither the daughters nor son had any affection for their father.

During the summer of 1875, the cheese factory was operated by George Boyd, assisted by his brother, William Boyd.

It did not take the brothers long before they heard about Colonel Thompson's miserly habits and the ill treatment of his son. Will Boyd became very sympathetic and friendly with Frank Thompson. The youth had never been farther from home than Earlville, Smyrna and Lebanon, and he enjoyed listening to Boyd's stories of the larger cities he had visited. Soon young Thompson was telling Boyd about his father's money that was kept in the house and the arrangement of the bedrooms where the family slept.

About July 15, after the flush of the milk was over, William Boyd quit work at the cheese factory and left the neighborhood.

Four husky men stepped down off the train in Randallsville on Tuesday night, August 3, 1875, and started walking leisurely along the tracks toward Earlville. At the Felt farm crossing they were met by William Boyd. Each had a single purpose; they were after Colonel Thompson's money.

At the Thompson home in the Lebanon hills, a short distance west of Earlville, Mrs. Thompson, who was a slight, frail woman was working. It was not until 11 o'clock that she put out the lamp and retired for the night.

She was still awake when one of the men suddenly appeared at her bedside. He warned her she would not be injured in any manner if she would keep quiet. Mrs. Thompson huddled silently in her bed. When the man left, he hooked her door on the outside.

Colonel Thompson was attacked in his bedroom by three men who surrounded his bed. Although he was 72 years old he put up a good fight before he was overpowered and tied hand and foot to the four bed posts. In the struggle, his pants which contained over $300 in a pocket, were kicked out of sight under the bed. The pants went unnoticed in the dim light of the room.

A loaded double-barreled shotgun the old man kept near his bed was handed to one of the men who stood guard outside the home.

Frank Thompson, in his nearby room, was also guarded. He was finally tied hand and foot to the bed posts.

With the robbers in full possession of the house, Colonel Thompson's trunk was opened and his money box taken from it. Some of the men took the box into the kitchen and placed it on the table. The $1,220 it contained was divided among the men.

The burglars acted leisurely. They went to the pantry and prepared a meal and ate. Afterwards, the men warned the family that if any of them appeared outside the home before daylight they would be shot. They locked the family in their rooms and left.

Colonel Thompson, after considerable effort, managed to free one hand and then untied himself. He quickly untied his son and freed his wife. The ropes had stopped the circulation in the boy's hands and feet and required several hours before it was restored.

The family was so thoroughly frightened they told no one of the robbery until four days had passed. In the search for clues by the sheriff, Thompson's shotgun was found in the deep grass by the nearby wayside. From Randallsville the robbers had taken a handcar and pumped it to Clinton where it was abandoned. The men made a clean get-away.

George Boyd took over the operation of the Charles Loomis Cheese Factory on the Handsome Brook. In 1877, his brother William visited him. He was recognized and word was sent to law officers in Earlville.

"Chet Corham and Celester Hayward organized a posse and came to the Loomis home," John Mulligan of Sherburne recalled. "They rushed the cheese factory on the double quick.

"George Boyd saw them coming around the corner and he rushed up the stairs to give the alarm. The posse was right at his heels. Bill Boyd awoke with bracelets on his wrists," Mulligan said.

Boyd was placed in the Norwich Jail. During his trial Frank Thompson testified that he recognized Bill Boyd's voice on the night of the robbery. He also claimed he was able to identify the pants Boyd had been wearing as they were patched by cloth of another color.

Boyd was convicted and sentenced to a term in Auburn Prison. He swore he would kill Frank Thompson when he got out.

"In due time he (Boyd) came back to his old stamping ground," Mulligan said. "I saw him shortly before he went 'over the road', back to prison a second time from Chenango County. This time he never returned.

On the 29th day of August, 1897 he died friendless and alone," Mulligan recalled. "On the following day, according to the custom of the friendless dead, his remains were delivered to Syracuse University for the benefit of medical science.

"I do not know whether Bill Boyd comes back from the land of the shades," Mulligan said, "but I do know his name was written high among the immortals of the Loomis Gang."

The Sherburne man said Boyd never did make good his threat to kill Frank Thompson.

The robbery of Colonel Thompson was a topic for conversation for many years. It has now passed into the realm of folklore.

While there was considerable sympathy for Mrs. Thompson and Frank practically none was wasted on the colonel.

Despite his ill treatment, Frank remained with his parents and operated the farm. Colonel Thompson died in 1887 at the age of 84 years and Mrs. Thompson in 1892. Frank died at the age of 78 in 1936. He is buried in the Earlville Cemetery.

THE CONKLIN BROTHERS

The Conklin brothers names rank high on the list of great Adirondack guides. Roscoe and Burton were sons of Henry Conklin, who represented the Town of Wilmert on the Herkimer County Board of Supervisors in the 1890's. The brothers were great hunters and spinners of folk tales. They possibly killed more bears than any other guides before or since. An old postcard photo of Burt Conklin shows him surrounded by about eight bears — all dead.

During the deer season, if Burt Conklin was not in the woods with a party, he could usually be found at his small hotel and gasoline station in the hamlet of Noblesboro in Herkimer County. A short, stocky man of some seventy odd years, he had gray hair and a heavy walrus mustache.

One time Burt caught an unusually large fish. He had it mounted and placed on a wall in the barroom of his hotel. When a guest noticed the fish, he would ask Burt about how it was caught.

"I caught that fish," Burt would say, "but there is quite a story that goes with it." The guest naturally was anxious to hear the story. The old man would light his pipe and suck on it a few times, before starting to speak.

"It was like this," Burt said. "Some time ago I went fishing down on West Canada Creek. I sat on the bank about twenty four hours and I didn't get nary a bite. I tried first one kind of bait, then another, but none of those fish would take a nibble at it.

"After the night passed, it was morning and then soon it was afternoon. By this time I was mighty hungry and pretty desperate, but I did not want to go home empty handed."

"As I was sitting there and the sun was starting to go down, I saw a meadow mouse nearby," Conklin said. "I laid my pole aside, killed the mouse and cut off it's tail. I put the tail on my hook for bait and threw my line into the water. Right away I got that big fish you see there on my wall, on my hook. I had some trouble landing it, but I finally pulled it in."

The listeners, thinking Conklin had ended his story, prepared to leave.

"Hold on there," Burt said, "That ain't all the story, not by a durnsite. The fish was mighty big and I had quite a job getting it home."

"My wife sure was tickled to see that big fish I caught and made me carry it out into the kitchen where she prepared to clean it for supper. She got out the butcher knife and slit the fish down the belly to clean out the insides. But when she slit it open, what do you think happened?"

The visitors were all leaning forward now, anxious to hear the ending. Burt took another slow drag on his pipe.

"It sure is mighty hard to believe," he said, but a young hen jumped out of that fish's belly, like Noah coming from out of the whale. That chicken laid an egg right there on the table.

"My wife was so flabbergasted she refused to cook the fish. She wanted it mounted to hang on the wall so everyone could see it."

Roscoe Conklin had a narrow escape from being killed by a wounded bear late in 1897. The story was carried by the Saturday Evening Globe on November 26, as reported by Conklin.

Roscoe said at the time he was employed by his brother helping to build a barn.

"We lacked stone to finish the basement and made arrangements to go early one morning to a stone quarry about three miles in the woods, near an old pulp mill," Roscoe said. "My brother was to take the team and wagon, crow bar and ax and I was to go from my house in the morning and meet him at the quarry at 8 o'clock."

"After eating breakfast the next morning I shouldered my gun and started. My wife said I had better take a few more shells as I might need them. I replied that I had plenty, supposing the magazine was full and off I went looking for game as I went along," he said.

At 8 o'clock I arrived at the quarry, but my brother had not arrived. I strolled around a little and finally sat down on a log on a little knoll from which position I could look over a large territory. I had been seated on the log only a few moments when I saw a flock of partridges flying toward me. It seemed as if they were frightened by something. One of them lit near me and I fired at it, cutting a few feathers off its breast.

"While I was looking at the birds my attention was drawn to a crashing in the brush where the birds came from and looking that way I saw a monstrous bear come loping towards me through the brakes and berry bushes. I said to myself, 'Mr. Bear, you are my meat and I will take you out with me on the wagon.' "

"When he was within 10 rods of me I took aim and fired," Roscoe said. "Instead of bringing down the bear I brought down a small sapling that was in the way. The charge cut the sapling off clean and I failed to hit the bear in the shoulder which I aimed at. The charge struck him somewhere, however, for he stopped and gave a loud growl as if in pain."

"He was standing on his hind legs with his forepaws on a log," Conklin remembered. "I took aim and fired a second shot. The ball struck a twig but it nearly cut one of his forelegs off at the shoulder. The leg was hanging by the skin only. Down went the bear, rolling and tumbling and gnashing his wounded leg."

Conklin said he thought he had the bear for certain. Deliberately walking up to within 12 feet of him, Conklin took good aim and pulled the trigger. Nothing happened. He worked the lever again and again. There was no sound. The woodsman pulled open the rifle and found it empty!

"Great Scott! I was in for it now for the wounded brute had discovered me," Conklin said. " With every hair on its back sticking forward, eyes flashing red, his tongue protruding, blood and foam coming from his mouth and giving unearthly growls, he made a leap for me!"

The woodsman did not hesitate. He turned and ran, his legs carrying him over logs and brush. Soon he was on the old pulp road.

"I glanced over my shoulder and saw that bear was close to my heels, gnashing his bloody jaws and grabbing at my heels and coat tail, while his bleeding leg was swinging from side to side," Conklin said. "I threw my useless gun away and then my coat and hat.

"I thought my last moment had come and my mind went back to my wife and the folks at home," the woodsman said. "Everything I had ever done went rushing through my mind. Again I glanced over my shoulder and the bear was still at my heels giving vent to such roars as never before came from a brute's mouth."

Coming around a bend in the road, Roscoe saw the camp and his brother, Burt. He waved his arms over his head, shouting for Burt to hurry.

"My brother seeing me and the bear, jumped to his feet and ran the team over the rough stony road, making a terrible racket," Conklin said. "When the bear caught sight of the team he turned off into the forest. I fell to the ground prostrate, in fact almost dead with fright."

After resting a few minutes from his close call, the brothers armed themselves with an ax and crowbar and started out on the bloody trail of the bear.

"We tracked him by a trail of blood and found out where he had laid down several times, Roscoe said. "On our approach he would get up and run. We obtained a glimpse of him several times, but after chasing him into the big swamp, we gave up the hunt. We concluded he was not mortally wounded.

"I found my gun, coat and hat," Roscoe said. "Then we loaded our stone and went home. I was almost sick with fright for several days.

"I wish to say, always take your wife's advice," he said. "Keep your gun loaded and never tackle a wounded bear with an empty gun. When I was running down that road with the bear at my heels, I could see the angels," he added.

A MAN NAMED MULLER

On top of one of the sheerest hills in Central New York, some two thousand feet above sea level, about half way between Georgetown and DeRuyter there is an overgrown circular roadway and the remains of a cellar wall. To this place in the summer time ten to fifteen carloads of visitors drive up the narrow, dusty road on weekends to explore and ponder over the mystery of Muller Hill.

In the spring of 1808, a Frenchman of royal bearing came to Payne's Settlement (Hamilton) with a woman, people believed to be his wife, and several servants. The couple also had a small boy with them, supposedly their son. The Frenchman, who remained aloof from the residents, used the name of Lewis Anthe Muller. His employees remained faithful to him, for none ever divulged his identity.

Since that time many writers and historians have attempted to penetrate the enigma of the seigneur of Slab City. He has been called the Duc d'Angouleme, the Duc de Berri and Charles X. The identity of the blond, American woman who came with him was called Eugenia Adaline Stuyvesant by Mrs. L. M. Hammond-Whitney, author of a Madison County history and several biographies. However, this was denied by John R. Stuyvesant on September 14, 1899, who said there was no Stuyvesant woman of marriageable age in 1808.

Muller was reported to have been about fifty years of age when the couple came to Payne's Settlement. He was about five feet, five inches in height, well proportioned, with a swarthy complexion and penetrating dark eyes. His features were sharply defined. His wife was younger, fair-haired, of medium height, well-formed and graceful.

During the French Revolution, many members of the royalty and others of high rank in the French Government, fled to the United States to escape the guillotine. Muller sometimes appeared to live in fear of Napolean Bonaparte. However, he followed Napolean's campaigns closely.

Before coming to Payne's Settlement, Muller had purchased 2,700 acres of forest land on the hilltop near Slab City (later Georgetown) from Daniel Ludlow of New York City, a land speculator. Muller paid $9,862.25 for the tract. It appears he wanted to live away from the communities where some of his enemies might recognize him. Muller was reported to be carrying $150,000 in gold and was guarded constantly by two armed men.

Muller also brought a letter of introduction with him when he came to Payne's Settlement. It was from Mr. Ludlow to Thomas M. Hubbard, a young lawyer, who had settled in the hamlet five years earlier.

The Frenchman and his retinue set out on horseback to see his property shortly after he had established lodgings in the Settlement. The party followed trails to Slab City, some twelve miles to the west. Slab City contained about six log houses.

Muller selected some 300 acres on a hill overlooking the settlement for the site of his home. He hired local woodsmen, laborers and artisians. The men built a road through the forest and cleared the trees and brush from the 300 acres. Every large stone and stump was removed. As soon as this was done, Muller picked the spot where he wanted his "chateau" built. It was to be beyond any rifle shot that could be fired from the woods.

The "chateau" was seventy feet in length and thirty feet in width and was a story and a half in height. The foundation enclosed a spacious stone cellar. The walls of the building were of solid black cherry timbers, eleven feet in length and twelve and eighteen feet broad. The timbers were placed upright and dovetailed into the massive girders and heavy sills. The outside was covered with clapboards and the interior was lathed and plastered.

A spacious hall, ten feet in width, ran the entire length of the building. On the left of the hall there was a bedroom, dining room, kitchen and pantry. There were seven large fireplaces, each with a black marble mantle.

The furnishings were shipped from France and carried to the chateau by packhorse. A piano and a library of finely-bound books were also packed in. They became the wonder of the workmen.

Three large barns were built near the house. A stream that ran near the house was dammed and stocked with fish. A deer park was built on the easterly slope where the descent to Bronder Hollow begins.

A circular drive led up to the chateau. Shrubbery and selected trees, including butternut and populars were used in the landscaping.

A stream of water meandering down into a small valley was dammed; a winding road cut along the side of the hill, leading down into the valley. A sawmill, gristmill, two stores, a warehouse and several homes for the workmen were built. Muller named the settlement Bronder Hollow in honor of John Passon Bronder, who had come with the seigneur and was overseer of the work. Muller offered inducements to the workmen to settle their families in the Hollow. Bronder and Del Camp, another Frenchman, kept the first store.

As soon as the chateau was ready for occupancy in 1809, Muller moved his family into it. They settled into their new home. Muller rarely left his estate, excepting to go to Payne's Settlement. He was friendly to the people he met, but never became intimate with any of them. Muller's only confidente was Dr. Petrow, his private physician, who came from France with him.

Residents of the area were aware Muller was a man of consequence. At this time there were hundreds of French refugees living in New York State and Pennsylvania. Many of them were royalty.

Angel DeFerrier, another wealthy, displaced Frenchman, resided on a smaller estate at Wampsville. He married Polly Denny, the daughter of John Denny, a trader at Canaseraga, and his Indian wife. DeWitt Hadcock of Stockbridge, a grandson of DeFerrier said the Frenchmen were well-acquainted with each other. Hadcock wrote in the early 1900's of a visit DeFerrier, his mother and Aunt Lucy made to Muller's chateau.

"When grandfather and Muller met they both embraced and kissed each other and then began to talk French, recalling the scenes of their early life," Hadcock wrote. He said nothing about Muller's actual identity.

Muller received dispatches from France at regular intervals and scanned them for information about Napolean. Whenever important news about the wars sweeping Europe arrived, the French seigneur would call his employees and read the dispatches to them.

A peddler is reported to have visited the chateau one night and was never seen again. There was gossip that the peddler was a spy in disguise and Muller had him shot. In later years some of Muller's employees told of a well being filled in. Other stories tell of an emissary from Napolean and a royal refugee being hidden by Muller to escape their enemies.

In 1812, when Muller learned Napolean was marching into Russia, he became greatly excited. He said it was the beginning of the end.

Only once during his residence on Muller Hill did the Frenchman give any indication of his past. This was about the time the new United States had gone to war with Great Britian. The militia captain at Hamilton, formerly Payne's Settlement, sent word for every able-bodied man to turn out for training. Muller was infuriated by the order. He was talking to his employees when the order was handed him. Muller read the message and lost his restraint.

"Mr. (Chancellor) Bierce, it is too bad, too bad," he said. "Captain Hurd sends his corporal to warm me out to train. He ought to be ashamed! I have been general of a division five years. I have signed three treaties. I . . ." Muller suddenly caught himself. He added shortly, "Bierce, it is too bad."

Muller liked to hunt and fish. A crack shot, he always believed in firing at game on the move. He rode horseback over his estate, accompanied by armed, mounted retainers.

Baccus White, an employee, told Henry Breed of Quaker Basin, several incidents about the Frenchman. Muller sent him on horseback to the gristmill and on other errands.

"He (White) said they had a bear chained up in front of the house in some way," Breed wrote. "The chain was long enough for the bear to get into the hall where there was a large looking glass which reached from the floor to the ceiling. Here bruin saw himself in the glass. Uncle Baccus said he knocked the glass in more than a thousand pieces.

At another time, the bear was chained in the front yard near the woodpile," Breed said. "The hired girl came out to get some wood. In some way she ventured too near the bear. The bear grabbed her and put his paws around her. It was soon life or death for the girl. Mr. Muller saw the affair, took down his rifle and shot the bear dead," Breed said.

"Muller went duck hunting one day on a pond just north of Georgetown, with his horse and two dogs," Breed recalled. "As he came where the pond was, a boy by the name of Abiather Hunt, let down the bars for him. He (Muller) rode up to the pond and sent his dogs out. They scared up some ducks, of which he shot two. The dogs brought them from the pond to the horse. They put their paws up against the horse and gave Mr. Muller the ducks without his getting out of the saddle," Breed wrote.

White told Breed many other stories about his employer.

"There was a man by the name of Alpheus Wood, who worked for Muller, as a woodsman," Breed said. "Muller got it into his head the men were not chopping quite enough to suit him. The men decided to do something about it. They found Muller one day watching them from the edge of the woods. So they cut the trees on the back side, half off, some of the large ones far back into the woods," Breed said White reported.

"Finally Muller came again, looking from behind the trees. The men started their back tree and one kept pushing the others over until the falling trees came so close to Muller, he had to run like a whitehead," Breed wrote. "Muller never was seen looking from behind a tree after that," he said.

Breed recalled his uncles, Elijah and Phineas Hunt and a man named Isaac Warren, worked for Muller.

Muller knew nothing about agriculture. The area that had been cleared on Muller Hill was unproductive. When the seigneur had his fishpond built, the workmen had leveled off the hardpan.

A story is told of Muller seeking seed to grow an acre of turnips. He asked a neighbor how much seed he should buy and was told three bushels." Muller had his men scour the countryside for three bushels of turnip seed.

One farmer asked Muller why he wanted all the seed. When he learned the Frenchman wanted to plant an acre, the farmer explained the joke that had been played.

Mrs. Muller gave birth to two children, a boy and a girl, while residing in the chateau.

When Napolean was defeated at Waterloo and banished to Elba in 1814, Muller was elated. Packing his bags and accompanied by his wife, children and personal servants, he left Muller Hill for New York City. The chateau and property were left in the hands of an agent.

Muller is said to have left his family in New York while he sailed for France.

In 1816, he returned to Muller Hill. The road from George-town and the carefully attended acreage were overgrown with the growth of two years. The chateau was empty and silent, its doors sagging open to the weather. The agent had stripped the building of its furnishings and departed. No trace of him could be found.

Muller returned almost at once to New York City and offered his property for sale. A New York merchant, Abijah Watson, bought the chateau, barns and grist mills and other property for $10,000. The deed signed April 9, 1816, with Cornelius Bogart and Jacob Radcliffe attesting. Radcliffe was mayor of New York.

The property changed hands many times during the ensuing years. One barn was destroyed by fire. The saw and grist mills had disappeared by 1825. The chateau also burned in 1905. In recent years the property has been taken over by the state and reforested.

Muller and his family disappeared as suddenly as they had appeared that day in Payne's Settlement. The subject has been one that puzzled amateur and professional historians alike.

Two novels have been written about the family. Each gave Mrs. Muller a lover whom she eventually married. There have been thousands of magazine and newspaper articles written. One serious amateur historian said Muller never returned to France. He lived and died in the state. His body lies in someone's front yard, the historian said. He refused to say where. His excuse was the public would overrun the place.

Muller and his family are a enigma. It is certain the seigneur of Muller Hill was a man of importance, if he was not of royal blood. Unlike Betsy Patterson, whom Joseph Bonaparte married and left, no one has ever come forward to tell what occurred to Adeline Muller or the couple's children.

To the end, the Frenchman must remain a man called Muller.

THE LORD PROVIDES

Old John Siver used to take to the woods with his fishpole and bony, flea-bitten dog, Ebenezer, to escape the scolding tongue of his wife, Sarah.

The elderly couple resided in a weather-beaten little house that stood near Sam Houpt's stone grist mill on the bank of Nowadaga Creek in Newville, during the early 1800's. Mrs. Seaver worried constantly about her empty cupboard. She kept her husband busy chore'n about the hamlet when he wasn't laid up with rheumatism. Old John, who like the fabled Rip Van Winkle, disliked work, sneaked away to the woods every chance he could.

One day Siver returned home from one of his chore'n jobs carrying an antique blunderbus. Mrs. Siver eyed her husband suspiciously over the top of her silver-rimmed spectacles as he entered the kitchen.

"John Siver, you old fool, where on earth did you get that rusty old thing?"

"What — this gun?" There was a touch of the naive in Old John's question.

"You call that rusty thing, a gun?" Sarah raised her hands in horror. "John Siver . . . tell me where did you get it?"

The old man grinned sheepishly as he fingered the wide barrel of the blunderbus. "Why, I done a mite of work for Doc Snyder this mornin' and when he was goin't to pay me, I says, 'Doc, if I can have that old musket you got in your garret, I'm willin' to call it square.' "

"An — then?" Mrs. Siver's mouth set in grim lines.

"That's all there is to it," John said. "Doc just gave it to me."

"You brainless old fool," Mrs. Siver's wrath descended on her husband like the sudden coming of a summer storm. ' Do you mean to say you refused good money — for that?"

"No, now, Sarah," Old Siver pleaded, as if attempting to stem the torrent, "There ain't nothin' to make such a fuss about."

"Make a fuss?" Mrs. Siver raised her hands. "Law's a' mercy, I'm ashamed of you. Here I slave day in, day out, while you traipse around with your old dog."

The old man slowly edged towards the kitchen door, clutching his prize blunderbus. "You know I'd work if I was able to," he said hastily. "Remember what the good Book says about the Lord provideth for all."

"I'll provide you!" Sarah shouted. Seizing the stout hickory broom from beside the fireplace, she brought the tied brush whisks down on her husband's head. "You git. I hope you blow your fool head off an' that dog's too."

When John Siver returned home that night, he was a changed man. For the next few months Sarah found little to complain about. John turned down an offer made by "Uncle Sam" Houpt to work in his grist mill. However, he did weed and hoe his garden and chopped a pile of kindling.

October came and the wind blew the dead leaves from the trees and rustled the drying corn stalks in the field. The frost lay white on the pumpkins in the fields. In the blue sky above there came the sound of geese flying southward.

Sarah Siver was feeling rather poorly. In her big bed in the kitchen, she shivered and drew the frayed quilts up over her thin chest for warmth.

"John . . . . John," she called. Her husband was sitting near the fireplace cleaning his blunderbus.

"Yes, Sarah?" he asked gently.

"You tinkerin' with that gun again?"

"I was thinkin' a fat goose might be good eatin' ", he said. "The grease might be good for your chest."

The old lady raised herself painfully on one elbow. "John, you ought to take that job at the mill. How are we goin' to eat?"

Siver laid his gun aside and rose stiffly from his chair. Approaching the bed he patted his wife's arm awkwardly. "Now, don't fret. The Lord will provide for us somehow."

Sarah burst into tears and turned toward the wall without answering. John studied his wife's back for a minute, then he returned to the table. Picking up his powder horn, he poured some into the barrel and rammed it down firm. Next he dropped in an assortment of old nails, bolts and screws and then rammed in a piece of cloth for wadding.

"I'll be back as soon as I get me a goose," he tried to make his voice cheerful, as he opened the door and went out. He whistled for Ebenezer. The dog came up unsteadily, wagging his stump of a tail. Siver and the dog walked toward the mill pond.

49

Old Siver sat partially hidden behind a tree stump for a considerable period before he heard a honking from the sky. Looking upward he saw a triangle of several hundred geese flying low, preparing to land. The old man and his dog sat motionless.

Minutes passed before the leader of the flock of geese settled on the pond followed by the others. Slowly old Siver rested his blunderbus across the stump and poured some powder in the pan. Taking aim at the geese, he pulled the trigger.

The whole valley vibrated with the roar. Old Siver was slammed backwards about a dozen feet. He picked himself up slowly, rubbing his shoulder. Dazedly he looked at the twisted ruin of his weapon. The body of the dog laid nearby. The air was filled with geese trying to escape.

The sun was painting the church and hotel below Firey Hill with gold, as John Siver slowly made his way home. He cautiously opened the kitchen door.

"It's about time you come home," Mrs. Siver spoke sharply from the bed. "There's nothin' in the house to eat for supper."

"Yes there is," Siver said proudly. "Look at what I got."

"Did you get a goose?"

"Better'n that, Sarah," the old man's voice was jubilant. "I got eleven geese. My old gun blew up and poor Ebenezer was killed. I guess now you'll believe me when I say, the Lord'll provide."

THE LOST SUPERINTENDENT

An Indian woman who was gifted with "second sight" is credited with helping to solve the mystery of a missing railroad superintendent.

Early in November, 1916, Carleton Banker of Gloversville, was one of seven executives of the Fonda, Johnstown and Gloversville Railroad, who went on their annual hunting expedition near Speculator. They made their headquarters at the camp of Truman Lawrence.

On Thursday, November 9, Banker and Frederick A. Bagg, the railroad's engineer, walked through the woods to the camp owned by David Brennan, a railroad man, who was supposedly hiding out from the law under the name of Foxey Brown. The three men went hunting the next day, and Banker shot a small deer. In the afternoon the superintendent's leg was bothering him, so he was stationed at the rear of a deer run. Bagg and Foxey went hunting. After spending the afternoon, Foxey decided to return to Banker, just as the sun started to set.

It was dark when Bagg finally met up with Brown. Banker was not with him. Bagg fired his rifle in the air. Very faintly in the distance they heard an answering shot. The two men were not worried as the railroad superintendent was an experienced woodsman. They returned to Foxey's cabin and prepared supper. They ate when Banker failed to show up, then later retired for the night.

On Saturday morning the men continued the search. Some footprints were seen. Bagg, who was worried, immediately started for Piseco seeking help.

Two separate parties began the search. On the following Sunday morning more than fifty men were in the woods. No sign of the missing man was found.

Mrs. Banker and her two daughters in Gloversville were notified.

By Monday the weather had turned colder and it started to snow. Bloodhounds were brought in to aid in the search, but they were unable to turn up any sign of the missing man. The next Wednesday afternoon, it was the general concensus of opinion that Banker was dead. A $6,000 reward was offered

51

for anyone finding him. State Police and veteran guides led the search, but with no results.

Banker was described as having a slight limp and wearing a gray hunting suit. He was wearing a large diamond ring that he had owned for over 23 years.

As the years passed suspicion focused on Foxey Brown and he moved away.

"Up here in Speculator, we folks don't forget such happenings easily," "Miz" George Perkins, wife of the forest ranger and guide remarked one fall night in 1931.

"Several years had passed when one day I heard of an old Indian woman in Gloversville named Mrs. Rays, who was said to be gifted with second sight. I became interested in the woman's gifts, especially when I heard of her aiding the Gloversville police in solving a murder case. I was determined to see and talk with her.

"I asked Mrs. Abrams and her son, Bill Abrams, who was one of the searchers for Mr. Banker, and who knew the Indian woman to go with me to Gloversville."

"We found the woman's home on Wells Street in the city," "Miz" Perkins said. "It was a ramshackled old building. I knocked loudly on the door but no one answered. Mrs. Abrams then knocked. The door slowly opened about an inch or so and a girl's deep voice asked fearfully, 'Who is it?'

"Mrs. Abrams and I want to see Mrs. Rays," I answered.

"You mean us no harm?" she inquired.

"No."

"After a moment's hesitation, the girl opened the door and permitted us to enter. In the dim hall light I looked at the girl. She was short, dark, with long straight hair, and was pleasant looking. She pointed to a doorway at the end of the hallway.

"My mother is in there," she said, and accompanied us into the next room. The room was barren looking. The Indian woman sat motionless, hunched deep in a heavy chair.

"Mother," the girl said, "people to see you."

"The hunched figure stirred. "You won't hurt us?" the old lady asked.

"We mean you no harm," I said. "Don't be afraid. We would like a reading."

"The old woman raised her head, and her piercing eyes studied our faces. Apparently satisfied, she waved a skinny arm toward some wooden chairs.

52

"Sit, sit."

"We sat close to her and waited for her to continue. Some minute spassed before Mrs. Rays nodded to Mrs. Abrams. 'Give me your hand,' she said and extended hers."

Mrs. Rays studied the lines of Mrs. Abram's palm, all the while muttering to herself. 'Place a half dollar in your hand,' she said. Mrs. Abrams did not have a half dollar in her purse but I had one and I loaned it to her."

" 'Close your hand,' the Indian woman directed, 'and hold the money tight.' "

"Mrs. Abrams squeezed the money until her knuckles turned white."

" 'Now make a wish.' "

"Mrs. Abrams nodded her head in assent, and the old woman clasped her hand once more."

" 'Now let me see your hand,' Mrs. Rays said."

"When Mrs. Abrams unclenched her fist, the Indian woman removed the coin and stared, as if fascinated at the imprint it had left. She then closed her eyes, swaying a little and muttering to herself, 'Oh, if my father were here. He could see so much.' Opening her eyes, she pointed a bony finger at Mrs. Abrams. 'You want to know about a man in a gray suit who disappeared a long time ago?' "

" 'Yes! Mrs. Abrams said breathlessly, while her son, Bill and I leaned suddenly forward."

" 'He wore a ring?' "

" 'Yes, yes.' "

" 'I see it sparkling, like a diamond,' the woman said, and then adding, 'This man limped?' "

" 'Yes.' "

" 'Like this —' Mrs. Rays arose nimbly from her chair despite her years and went around the room limping heavily with her left leg. Bill Abrams grabbed my arm. He was tense with excitement."

" 'My God,' his voice was strained, 'That is how Mr. Banker walked. I can never forget that.' "

"Mrs. Rays returned to her chair and sat down. She took Mrs. Abrams' hand again and examined the palm once more. 'Is this man still alive?' Mrs. Abrams asked. 'No,' the Indian woman answered, 'he is dead.' "

" 'Will he ever be found?' Mrs. Arbams inquired. The woman shook her head slowly. 'No, not for a long time,' she said."

"Mrs. Abrams plucked nervously at the bar pin on the collar of her dress. 'Where will he be found?' Mrs. Rays passed a quivering hand over her eyes and appeared to sink deeper into her chair. 'I can't see,' she almost moaned 'It is so hard for me to see. Oh-h my head . . .' "

" 'Please . . . please try to see,' Bill Abrams begged."

"The Indian woman rocked her body from side to side, as if the penetration into the future was causing her great agony. 'I-I-see . . . . something shiny. I-I can't describe it. The sun strikes it and it shines.' "

" 'Is that all?' "

" 'I see the man laying near the road,' Mrs. Rays continued slowly. 'He is in a deep hole and covered. I-I can't see anymore. There is nothing more . . . Go-go,' she waved us away."

"Awed and shaken at what had been revealed to us, we arose. We paid Mrs. Rays daughter her mother's fee, and then stumbled from the dark interior of the house out into the warm sunshine."

"When I reached home I told George, my husband about our experiences. He laughed and said we must have been dreaming. Mrs. Abrams and her son wisely kept what they had learned to themselves. As the days passed, and then the weeks and months, I too, began to wonder if I had been dreaming. Eventually it all slipped from my mind."

"One day the unexpected occurred. Just six years later, on Friday, November 10, 1922, Bill Abrams was hunting north of Piseco Lake. He was a short distance from the Spruce Lake trail when his dog started growling and pawing at a small patch of leaves. Thinking the dog had found a woodchuck hole, Bill called to the dog. The animal was usually obedient, but this time, he ignored his master and kept pawing at the leaves. Bill lost his patience, and reached over to pick the dog up by the scruff of the neck. Something shiny reflected into his eyes. He picked up a weathered Prince Albert tobacco can on which the sunshine had glinted.

"Bill said later he suddenly remembered what Mrs. Rays had told us that day in Gloversville 'I-I see something shiny, but I-I can't describe it.' "

"Excitedly he began kicking about in the pile of leaves and dirt until he found a human skull. Nervously he used the butt of his rifle to scrape away the dirt. More bones were uncovered. He turned up a leg and an arm bone, the barrel of a rifle, whose stock had been eaten by animals, a gold watch and a diamond ring. Bill put the watch and ring in his pocket and stumbled out onto the road a few feet away.

The objects were identified by Carleton Banker's two daughters, Helen and Marian Banker, and by his attorney, William Baker as belonging to the missing railroad superintendent.

His body had been discovered about five miles from where he had been left. Several empty shells scattered about the bones indicated he had fired his rifle to attract attention.

"Bill Abrams received the award for finding the body," Miz Perkins said.

"I never have been back to visit the Indian woman," she remarked humorously, "She knows too much. I would rather not know what will happen to me."

"FATHER" BETTINGER'S FAMILY

Martin Bettinger was a kindly man, admired and respected by his neighbors and Indians alike, who nicknamed him "father".

When there was trouble between any of the German or English settlers in the neighborhood of the Minden area in the Mohawk Valley, he would try to arbitrate by bringing the antagonists together before they had a chance to come to blows.

Father Bettinger's favorite saying was, "Let not the sun go down on your wrath," which he quoted from the Bible. But, whenever any of his grandchildren were misbehaving, all his daughters had to say, was "Wait until Father Bettinger comes," and the children at once were calm.

Father Bettinger was a devoted Christian and an active member of the old Lutheran Church of Minden when the Rev. Christopher Wheeting was pastor.

Small in size and with a birthmark on his face, Bettinger was born in the Duchy of Wurtemberg in August, 1734. His mother Frau Anna Christina Bettinger, had a sore on her leg, and the doctor told her he thought if she would go to the American Colonies she might be cured. However, the doctor said, if her leg healed while on the boat, she would die.

Taking his advice, Frau Bettinger sailed for America with her son, Martin, who was fifteen. During the six-month voyage his mother's leg began to heal. She tried to irritate it by using wood ashes and gunpower. She died when the leg healed and was buried at sea. The youth found he was alone.

(The family story is somewhat different from the official records that state Martin Bettinger came to America in the second Palatine migration. According to the 1790 census: List of poor Palatinates who arrived in St. Catherin's, June 2, 1709. Third arrivals from Germany to England — Anna Christina Bettinger, widow, age 60, with son (possibly grandson), age 9, daughters, 17-4 — Church, Reformed.)

Nothing further was known of his activities after reaching the New World until he married Magdalena Keller. At the time the fires of the Revolution began to spread, they lived with his family at Dutchtown at Fort Willett, in the neighborhood of Minden.

Father and Mrs. Bettinger were always considerate of their neighbors and no Indian was ever turned away from their double cabin. One night a dignified Mohawk chief sat at their table and spent the night with the family. He was Joseph Brant, better known as Thayendangea.

When the flames of war spread into the Valley, the Bettingers, like their neighbors lived in constant fear of the Indians and Tories. General Nicholas Herkimer heard that St. Leger was on his way to attack Fort Stanwix. He called for volunteers and the Tryon County militia to go to the relief of the Fort. Men between the ages of sixteen and sixty were urged to enter the service, while those over sixty years were called upon to defend the women and children.

Father Bettinger was forty-five years of age. He enlisted in the First Canajoharie District Regiment under Colonel Ebenezer Cox. The regiment joined with General Herkimer's and on August 4, 1777 started to the relief of Fort Stanwix.

On the morning of the sixth the militia reached the junction of the Oriskany Creek and the Mohawk River. General Herkimer wanted to stop and dispatch scouts, but Colonel Cox and Captain Issac Paris insisted upon pressing forward. They called the general a "coward". Herkimer angrily gave the command "Forwarts." A few minutes later the valley militia was caught in the murderous ambush.

Father Bettinger survived the battle, and returned to Fort Herkimer with the survivors. Brant, his Indians, Butler's Rangers and Tories began raiding the settlements in the Valley, in the fall of 1781.

Early one morning as Mrs. Bettinger was working about her home in Dutchtown, a shadow fell across the doorway. Startled, she glanced up and saw Joseph Brant standing there.

He motioned for Mrs. Bettinger and her children to follow him, and as they walked away, he explained that the Indians were on the warpath and would be there within an hour.

Magdalena Bettinger and her children followed, the youngest clinging to her skirts in terror. Brant led them a mile or two away from the trail and hid them. He told them to remain and not to leave under any circumstances, until he came for them.

Mrs. Bettinger suddenly realized that her six-year old daughter, Christina, was not with her. The child had been out of sight playing when the family had left with Brant. The mother had an almost uncontrollable desire to go after her daughter, but remembered the lives of her smaller children depended upon her.

As dusk came, Brant returned and told them they must remain hidden. The baby was crying softly for water. Chief Brant told Mrs. Bettinger to take the scissors she carried in her belt and dig into the soft soil with them. The mother did and the hole filled with water.

At sundown the Indian chief returned and led them back to their cabin, one of the few left standing. Christina was gone. Brant said she had been carried off by one of his Mohawks.

Jacob Bronner, his son, Christian and daughter, Sophronia, were taken prisoner at the same time.

Father Bettinger was later reunited with his family. He learned Christina was with the Mohawks in Canada. After the war he went to Brantford, Canada seeking his daughter. Bettinger found her. In appearance and dress, Christina was a typical Indian. She had been taken as a wife by a Mohawk scout. The couple had two children.

Father Bettinger identified her from a dogbite scar on her arm. He begged her to return home with him, but her warrior would not go. Christina cried when her father gave her a cake her mother had baked for her, but refused to leave.

Father Bettinger returned to his cabin in Dutchtown.

The family later moved to Brookmens Corners where Father Bettinger and his wife spent the remainder of their lives, in the peace he had fought for.

FRENCHMEN OF THE CHENANGO

The foliage was turning red and gold on the eastern side of the Chenango River, when Charles Felix Bue Boulogne of France first saw it. He obtained a deed for 15,360 acres of land on October 9, 1792, from Malachi Treat and William V. Morris. They had received the letter of patent from the State of New York, August 13, 1787.

Boulogne paid a small amount of cash on his purchase, and executed a mortgage to Treat and Morris for 614 pounds. He started seeking French settlers for his land.

The property was within the present limits of the Village of Greene. Hundreds of royalists and upper middle class gentry sought refuge in the new United States when the revolution swept like a plague across their homeland. The majority went to Philadelphia, Pa. From there they bought property on the Susquehanna and founded Azilum, (or Asylum) and prepared for the escape of King Louis XVI and Queen Marie Antoinette and their family. They started the Scioto colony on the Ohio River, and also settled at Chaumont, Cape Vincent, DeFeriet, and other locations in northern New York State.

Boulogne brought the first settlers to his colony shortly afterwards. They were M. Shamont, M. LeFevre, M. Bravo, M. Duvernet and M. Obre with their families, including several young ladies and children. These families took a long circuitous way to their new homes in the wilderness, going to New York City, thence to Albany and Schenectady, and finally up the Mohawk River to Fort Plain. The Frenchmen are believed to have struck from the Mohawk Valley to the Town of Butternuts in Otsego County. At Butternuts they were joined by Simon Barnett, who was born in Martinique, West Indies, of French parents. Barnett came to Philadelphia during the American Revolution, and after peace was declared, exchanged his property there for land in Otsego County. He moved to Butternuts with his wife, Margaret Sidell, a German girl he met in Phildelphia.

At the age of fourteen, Barnett started for the United Colonies in a French privateer. He was captured by a British man-of-war and brought to Philadelphia, where he escaped.

Barnett learned the trade of ship's carpenter. He saved money until he was able to purchase a house and lot in Philadelphia. Barnett, who had a knowledge of English, contracted with Stephen Ketchum to cut a road through the wilderness from the site of their settlement to the "Chenango Road", at a point where the east line of the present town of Greene intersects it. Ketchum came from Ballston in 1792 and built a cabin in Greene. Members of the party and their families enjoyed the hospitality of Ketchum's cabin while building their shelters.

Under the directon of Boulogne the village site was laid out on the east bank of the river. Each lot contained 10 acres, and the entire settlement about 300 acres.

The Frenchmen planned to carry on farming as it was done in their native land, with the farmer and his family residing in the village, but owning and working on his farm in the adjacent county.

All were ladies and gentlemen of education and refinement without knowledge of building a cabin or grubbing the soil around the tree stumps to plant for much needed corn, wheat and potatoes. The men put up cabins and shelters for their families. Provisions and supplies were brought in from great distances with much labor and expense.

After the settlement was started, M. Dutremont joined it. He was a gentlemen of comparative wealth and talent and was acquainted with Charles Maurice Talleyrand, formerly bishop of Autun, who was exiled by the pope for his activities in confiscating church property. Talleyrand visited the settlement in August or September, 1794, accompanied by Mr. de Beaumetz, and an English millionaire named Lord, from India. The party came on horseback and remained a few days, then left for Albany. Talleyrand took a fancy to M. Dutremont's eldest son, and persuaded his parents to permit the youth to accompany him to France. Later young Dutremont became his private secretary.

Boulogne was enroute to Phildelphia in the spring of 1795 when he was drowned while fording the Loyal Sock, a tributary of the Susquehanna River. His leadership was greatly missed. Payments on their land were not kept up. Foreclosure proceedings on the mortgage were started in September, 1796, against Marie Victoria de Boulogne, his widow and heir. Through a final court decree on March 2, 1799, the lands reverted to Treat and Morris, the original vendors.

Loss of the property served as a death blow to the colony. The majority of settlers left in 1796, traveling down the Susquehanna into Pennsylvania where they joined their countrymen at Azilum. Mme. de Boulogne returned to France.

Captain Joseph Juliand joined the colony early in 1796, before its final break-up. The same year he was selected as an officer of the old Town of Bainbridge. Born in Lyons, France on January 17, 1749, he received a good education. His subsequent studies were directed toward becoming a medical practitioner. Captain Juliand abandoned his medical studies when he went to sea.

He rose through the ranks until he became a commander in the mercantile marine. Captain Juliand made several voyages across the Atlantic between the ports of Nantes and Bordeaux, France, and Boston and Phildelphia. These periodic visits furnished an opportunity for him to make trips into the interior of the eastern states, and to mingle with the people and learn English.

On one of these trips he became acquainted with Hannah Lindsley, the daughter of a New Haven, Connecticut farmer. They were married in 1788. Shortly afterwards they moved to a farm near Greenfield, Massachusetts.

Hearing of the French colony at Greene, he started through the unbroken wilderness to reach it. Leaving his family at Coventry, he pushed on to the settlement. Captain Juliand was disappointed to find several of his countrymen had pulled up stakes and left.

Juliand later purchased a considerable portion of the colony's land. When he died five sons and a daughter in the area survived him. For many years the Juliand Bank of Greene was a well-known institution.

Madame D'Antremont and her three sons who had joined the Asylum Colony in 1794, returned to Butternuts, and afterwards moved to Angelica, N. Y. Barnett and his family obtained 100 acres of land from Treat and Morris, located about four miles south the French settlement, and spent most of the rest of their lives there.

In March, 1838, when Barnett was at an advanced age, he moved to the home of his son, Charles Felix Bo Lyne Barnett, where he died.

Within a few years all vestiges of the settlement had disappeared, except traces of the road which remained to show where the French had tried to found a village in the wilderness of the Chenango.

THE OLD SOLDIERS

The old Revolutionary War veterans of Oxford used to gather at Well's Tavern several times a week for a mug of ale and a pipe of tobacco. Their discussions of their engagements would often grow heated.

The old red tavern was built in 1796. Of typical New England architecture, it was two stories in height in the front, with the rear at a slope so a man could touch the eaves. Behind the tavern was a large roofed shed with open sides to give some protection to the wagons and carriages during snow or rain.

The tavern rooms were low, studded with great beams. The wide, hard oak floors were worked smooth and white from sanding. There was a cavernous fireplace in the taproom. During the winter huge logs were dragged in to feed the flames. Behind the bar were rows of two quart pots, pint pots, gill pots, glass bottles and tankards. Tables and comfortable chairs were placed about the room. Against the walls were red settees and a large bunk on which the weary travelers spent the night, or the village loafer occupied during the day.

On this particular November afternoon, the old soldiers and a few townsmen were sitting in the barroom sipping their ale and smoking the long, clay, pipes, called "churchwardens" which they rented from the landlord.

Among them were Anson Cary, wearing his new broad-cloth suit and expensive shirt front; Eleazer Smith, who was tall and lanky; John Fitch, who had on his tile hat and stiff black stock; Josiah Hackett, in his continental suit; John Holmes and Jared Hinckley, both in homespun. All had served during the war.

As usual the talk drifted around to the Continental Army and some of its good officers and bad. John Fitch motioned to the landlord.

"Wells, bring me a pint of ale please, and a churchwarden," he said.

As Wells went to draw the ale, Fitch shifted in his chair, and started to talk about Benedict Arnold, who had betrayed the cause.

"Although rendered infamous by his attempt to betray his country —" he began, but was quickly interrupted by Hackett, He said loudly, "Rabbit ye, an' be darned. Hold your gab there. Old Arnold was a traitor."

"Yes, yes," Fitch said hastily, "but I want to say some things about him that I know. I was at the second battle at Freeman's Farm where the British were totally defeated by Arnold, who charged with mad fury upon their line."

He paused to accept the clay pipe from the landlord, lighted it with a taper, and then continued: "During the battle a wounded Hessian soldier lying on the ground fired at Arnold, and slew his horse. The ball passed through the general's left leg that had already been wounded, and fractured the bone above the knee. As Arnold fell, one of our men attempted to bayonet the Hessian, but the general cried out, 'For God's sake don't hurt him. He's a fine fellow!' The Hessian was spared. I have always said that was the time Benedict Arnold should have died."

"Oh, the old sneezer," Hackett exclaimed, "I've always heard when he was dressed up, the bottom of his waist was pinched up to the size of a quart cup, that he wore eleven capes to his coat, and over the place where his brains should have been, he wore a jockey cap of catskin. I understand he also carried a mock gold watch with two seals, each as big as a premium turnip."

"Old Arnold was quite a fop at that," John Holmes remarked, as he knocked the ashes from his churchwarden. "I have heard that before his death in England, he was shunned and despised by even the English."

A few of the veterans' pipes had gone out. There was quiet in the taproom as they knocked out the ashes, refilled and lighted them again. Fitch ordered a round of ale. After a few sips, Jared Hinckley started to recall one of his experiences.

"If ever I struck hell upon earth it was at the battle of Oriskany," he said slowly. "We fought in a dark ravine filled with a mass of fifteen hundred human beings, made up of St. Leger and his Indians and loyalists, and General Herkimer with 800 pioneers, all screaming and cursing, slipping in the mire, pushing and struggling, seizing each other's throats, stabbing and shooting, and dashing out brains."

"It was a sight that will never leave my eyes," Hinckley shuddered slightly. "General Herkimer had unconsciously marched into ambuscade, but his men soon recovered and fought with the courage and skill of veterans. The slaughter was dreadful.

"At the beginning of the battle a musket ball passed through and killed the horse of General Herkimer and shattered his own leg just below the knee. With perfect composure and cool courage, he ordered the saddle taken from his slaughtered horse and placed against the trunk of an immense tree, where he was carried and propped up. After lighting his Dutch pipe, he continued in a loud voice shouting orders to his men, who were falling like autumn leaves. But the old hero fought his last battle. His shattered leg was not skillfully treated and he died ten days later, propped up in bed, smoking his pipe and reading his Bible at the thirty-eighth psalm."

"It was after this battle that the first American flag with stars and stripes was raised," Anson Cary remarked.

"Yes, indeed," Hinckley replied, "though a crude affair it was."

"How so?" Eleazer Smith suddenly spoke up. He was always a good listener, but seldom expressed an opinion.

"Well, I'll tell you, "Cary picked at an imaginary piece of lint on his coat. "Not a great while before this battle, Congress had adopted the stars and stripes as the national symbol of American liberty. Colonel Willet returned to Fort Stanwix and raised five captured British standards, while over them he raised a hastily made flag to represent the American banner. It was made out of an old officer's white shirt and an old blue overcoat, and some stripes of red cloth from the petticoat of a soldier's wife. And that was the first American flag with stars and stripes hoisted."

Josiah Hackett nodded.

"Well, the English rigadoons scampered along through mud and mire to get out of sight," he said, "but it still waves over our land, and will till time is no more."

"Well spoken, Josiah," said John Holmes. "We'll take a final sip and go home. The hour is getting late."

The old veterans slowly pushed back their chairs and struggled to their feet. They hollered to Wells to mark down their tab, and started through the door into the cold. Hackett brought up the rear. As he closed the door, those in the taproom could hear his quavering voice raised in song:

"Yankee Doodle, ramrods, guns,
 Pikes and pistols handy —
We're the true descendant sons
 Of Yankee Doodle dandy."

OLIVER CURTIS PERRY — BANDIT

For years it was a popular sport for boys of Utica to search for Perry's cave in the hills near the city. It was the belief that money had been hidden in the cave.

Oliver Curtis Perry was Upstate New York's Jessie James, Butch Cassidy or the Sundance Kid back in the 1890's. Perry was a train robber.

The son of Irish immigrants, who came to the United States in the 1850's during the potato famine, Perry spent his early years working on his family's small farm at St. Johnsville, He was restless and resented parental discipline. Perry was in a reformatory at the age of 14, serving time for burglary.

He was to spend thirty eight years of his life in prison, thirty seven of them in wards for the criminally insane and twenty five in solitary confinement.

Perry did not look like a train robber or criminal. He was undersized, hollow-chested and almost effeminate. When he donned his gold-rimmed spectacles on his holdups, Perry looked like a church deacon or Sunday School teacher. His mild mannerisims and outward shyness were only a pose. Superintendent Bangs of the Pinkerton Detective Agency, called Perry, "the most dangerous criminal of our time."

In 1891, Perry worked as a yard man for the Fitchburg Line in Troy for $2 a day. He also joined the Presbyterian Church. A hard worker, he neither drank nor smoked. He devoted himself to church work. When called upon at his Troy boarding house, Perry would be found reading copies of The Fireside Companion or Golden Days.

The roistering, hard-drinking men of the railroad yards made Perry the butt of their jokes. He took it all mildly while he planned his first train robbery.

During his summer vacation he had made a fine-pointed saw in a farm workshop outside of Troy. He bought a gimlet in Amsterdam and purchased a revolver under an assumed name in a nearby town.

Perry had planned to hold up the American Express Company Special. He knew it was the most difficult train to tackle. It ran over the New York Central-Hudson line every night carrying currency and jewelry between New York City banks and western banks. The train often carried more than $1,000,000 in treasury notes. Perry knew the train was heavily guarded, but he was prepared.

He entered the Troy yards after midnight, September 29, 1891. When the Express train pulled in, he boarded it from the off side, between the money car and the passenger train. As soon as the train started, Perry removed the gimlet from his pocket and applied it to the solid door of the money car. Next he inserted his saw. The sound of the train and rocking cars covered his work. Within 15 minutes Perry had cut a hole in the doorway, large enough for him to enter.

Herbert Moore, the messenger, worked sorting packages and bundles by kerosene lantern. His revolver lay nearby. Perry adjusted his mask, set his derby at an angle and fired a shot over Moore's head.

The messenger jumped in surprise. Before he could recover, Perry jammed him in the ribs with his revolver. The mild bandit removed two packages of bills from the table and stuffed them inside pockets he had sewn in the outside coat. He picked up Moore's revolver and backed toward the hole he had cut in the door.

"If you try to follow me," he warned, "I'll blow your brains out the minute you stick your head through this opening."

Later Perry told the Pinkerton's the messenger acted sensibly. If he moved, "I'd have killed him," he said.

Before the train reached Utica, Perry cut the brake air lines. As the train ground to a stop, Perry leaped into the darkness. His trousers caught on a projecting rail guard and were practically ripped off. When he fell on the ground, his derby dislodged and he rolled on it. These unexpected events Perry had not forseen. He was to bemoan these until his death.

He realized it would be no use to try to return to his boarding house in Troy. His appearance would call for an explanation. Perry knew he could not enter a local store and buy trousers and a hat, as his appearance might mean instant arrest.

The bandit decided to go west. He traveled by night and hid during the day. The Pinkertons were able to obtain a good description of Perry from Moore, the men in the Troy yards and from his boarding house. They were on his heels throughout the west, yet never caught up with him.

Perry's haul from the train robbery only amounted to a small part of what he expected. He had run the risk for only $5,000, when he expected between $50,000 and $100,000.

Perry did not settle down to a quiet, domestic life he had mapped. Within five weeks he had spent most of the money on women and gambling. He began planning a second robbery. Perry started east toward New York State.

He boarded the Special at Rome on Sunday morning, February 2, 1892. The train was supposed to be carrying more than $1,000,000 in cash. Perry had not planned on the snow that covered the landscape. Under his overcoat, he had a rope ladder, hooked at one end, wrapped around his body. He sat for a time in a passenger car reading a newspaper. After awhile he laid down the paper and left the car.

The money car was the seventh from the end of the eight-car train. Dan T. McInerney, the messenger, worked alone in the car. Usually on the big Saturday night-Sunday morning run, two messengers were on duty.

Perry climbed onto the icy roof of a car and carefully crawled along the top. The strong wind from the fast-moving train was cold. He had all he could do to keep from being blown off.

When he reached the money car, he removed his rope ladder and hooked it under the eaves over the side door of the car. He lowered himself until he was able to look through the door window. When he saw McInerney cross to the other side of the car, Perry removed his revolver from his pocket and smashed the window with the butt. Thrusting the gun through the window, he aimed it at the messenger. McInerney went for his revolver and Perry shot it from his hand, damaging two of the messenger's fingers. Perry reached through the hole in the window and unlocked the door. When he swung the door open and leaped inside the car, McInerney tackled him. The two men rolled around the floor until Perry placed his gun against the messenger's thigh and pulled the trigger.

McInereny let go. Perry said if he made another move, he would kill him. The messenger begged for his life. McInerney was allowed to rise and to relight the kerosene lamp. He managed to pull the bell rope as he lighted the match.

The messenger was unable to open the safe because of his smashed fingers. Under his direction, Perry opened it. Great to the bandit's disappointment, there was no money in the safe, only jewelry.

Perry was enraged. He probably would have shot McInerney again if the train did not slow down as it reached Jordon, about seventeen miles west of Syracuse. The bandit leaped from the car into the snow and started running toward the locomotive. He fired a shot at the head of Caleb Cherry, who was at the throttle. The bullet missed. The train started up again. As the train passed, Perry climbed up onto the rear of the express and hid. When the train reached Lyons, the bandit managed to leave unseen. He started to mix with the crowd, but was spotted by Emil Laaso, the conductor of the special. Laaso remembered the bag Perry was carrying.

As the crowd began to advance, Perry ran across the tracks and leaped into a locomotive that stood with steam up, on the tracks. The bandit forced the fireman from the cab, then put it in gear and began driving the locomotive westward. He fired two shots at the crowd to keep them back.

The train crew and armed guards started in pursuit in the locomotive of the Special. Perry allowed the pursuing locomotive to draw close, then fired two shots through its cab window. The bandit then threw his locomotive in reverse and started backing toward Lyons.

The steam was running low in the locomotive and Perry was afraid that when he reached Lyons, he would be switched to a siding. Several miles from Lyons, Perry stopped the locomotive and leaped from it and started running towards the woods. He stole a horse from a farmer and rode off. About two miles further, he took another horse and cutter from a second farmer.

Perry was traced by officers and armed farmers led by Deputy Sheriff James Collins. The bandit was finally found behind a stone wall. Perry held them off for a while but was finally forced to surrender.

He was tried and sentenced to Auburn Prison on May 12, 1892. A year later Perry was judged insane and transferred to Mattewan Hospital for the Criminally Insane.

Perry remembered the judge who sentenced him saying he would remain in prison, "as long as you can see." After many months of experiments, Perry fashioned a device, using a dumbbell and needles, and blinded himself.

He was enraged when he was not turned loose.

The doctors and guards finally gave him up as hopeless. He often tore his clothes off and sat naked in his cell. He went on a hunger strike from 1903 to 1907 and was kept alive by forced feeding.

Sometimes he talked with reporters about freedom, which always seemed within reach.

Perry died in prison on September 10, 1930 and his spirit was free at last. He was buried in the prison hospital at Dannemora.

ADAM HELMER'S RUN

It was late in the afternoon when Adam Helmer reached Fort Herkimer. The sinking sun had already cast a bloody shadow over the valley.

Helmer's clothing was in tatters and his hands, face and body bleeding from the lacerations caused by thorny brush. His eyes were bloodshot and he gasped for air.

"The Indians are coming," he gasped. After delivering his message to the commander, he found a pallet and was instantly asleep. He slept for thirty six hours.

Joseph Brant, Captain Walter Butler and their tories and Indians had been expected in the German Flatts that summer of 1778. Colonel Peter Bellinger ordered Helmer, who was his son-in-law, and three other scouts, to travel as far as the Percifer Carr farm near the Unadilla River at Mount Edmeston, looking for signs of the enemy.

Mr. and Mrs. Carr were loyalists. Carr, who was employed by Colonel Edmeston, was a good friend of Brant's. He often supplied the Indians and tories with food.

When Helmer and the other scouts reached the Carr farm about 10 o'clock in the morning, they were surprised by some of Brant's Mohawks. The three scouts were killed. Helmer escaped by hiding in the brush. While the Indians searched, he saw a chance and started running. Helmer kept to the woods as much as possible to keep from being seen.

Fear for himself and the settlers of German Flatts lent wings to the 24-year old scout's feet. Helmer was about five feet, ten inches in height and weighed about one hundred and seventy five pounds. His constant outdoor life kept him in good physical condition.

Helmer swung west of Canadarago Lake, swinging away from Tunnicliff's, who were also friends of Brant and the British and avoiding the trail he and the other scouts had used. Across fields, the marshlands and through the brush, he ran. Once he came upon a party of about 200 Indians. Some of them started in pursuit, but Helmer outdistanced them.

At every settler's cabin he shouted to the occupants to get to the forts as fast as they could . . . . the Indians were coming.

The day passed slowly as Helmer kept running. He reached Andrustown and stopped at the home of his sister, Mrs. Maria Helmer Hoyer. She offered him something to eat, but he refused, afraid it would give him cramps. He did put on a new pair of moccasins to replace the worn ones he was wearing.

After seeing his sister and her family on their way to the fort, Helmer started running toward Columbia to spread the alarm. He finally reached Fort Herkimer and reported Brant and his Indians were coming.

Through Helmer's warning, the German families who lived in the vicinity of Fort Herkimer and Fort Dayton left their homes, livestock, furniture and crops and hurried to the forts for protection.

There were an estimated 152 Indians and 310 tories with Brant and Captain Butler. If they had struck Fort Herkimer at once, they might have overrun it. They were unaware Helmer had warned the countryside.

It started to rain that night. The Indians and tories camped in a small ravine not far from Shoemaker's Tavern (present Mohawk).

The next morning Brant and Butler attacked the fort and were driven off. The Indians and tories started running from cabin to cabin in the area, firing them, the barns and haystacks. The settlers watched helplessly from the fort as their work of many years went up in smoke. An estimated 125 buildings were destroyed. The raiders burned 63 houses, 57 barns, four mills, with the grain and furniture across the river. They also ran off 235 horses, 229 cattle, 269 sheep, 93 oxen and a number of hogs.

All that was left standing around Fort Herkimer was the church and two houses.

As soon as Adam Helmer had rested and eaten, Colonel Bellinger sent him with about 400 militiamen in pursuit of Brant and Butler. When they reached the Carr home in Mount Edmeston, they found the bodies of the stripped and scalped scouts and buried them.

The Oneida Indians, incensed over the Mohawks and tory raid on the valley, invaded the Carr home. They killed the servants and made captives of Mr. and Mrs. Carr.

Before the militia arrived, the Carr's and their servants managed to bury their dishes, silverware and some coins.

Helmer, who was promoted to lieutenant for his service to his country, served until the end of the war. He moved with his family to the Kingdom, a small hamlet south of Mohawk.

Mrs. Helmer, the former Anna Bellinger, was the daughter of Colonel and Mrs. Bellinger. They were married February 27, 1776 by the Rev. Abraham Rosencrantz, in the German Flatts Reformed Church. The couple had ten children. Two of the children were babies when Helmer made his run.

As a result of his military service, the government gave him a soldier's grant in the Town of Victory, Cayuga County. In 1804 the family moved to the Town of Brutus and built a cabin. Lt. Helmer, his wife and some members of his family are buried nearby.

A monument to the memory of the famous scout was dedicated in September, 1937, in the church yard of the Old Fort Herkimer Church. It honors him for his famous run that saved the lives of many of the settlers.

THE HANGING OF ROXY DRUSE

The metallic tones of the clock chimed eleven, that morning in the Herkimer County Jail, February 28, 1887. Mrs. Roxalana Druse shivered slightly in her cell. In a few minutes she was to hang for the murder of her husband, William Druse.

She could hear the men in the passageway below as the executioners were making a last inspection of the gallows. Mrs. Druse did not know one of the men mercifully drew a sliding door in the shed to hide the coffin waiting for her body.

At 11:31 Sheriff Delaven L. Cook with the physicians and deputies entered her cell. Mrs. Druse, who was seated in the low rocking chair with her back to the window, gave a sudden start. She paled, realizing her time had come. Mrs. Orasmus Waterman, a member of the death watch, laid a hand on her shoulder while the Rev. Dr. G. W. Powell whispered a brief word of comfort. As Mrs. Druse was assisted to rise, Mrs. Waterman threw a shawl about the woman's shoulders.

As the death march started, Mrs. Druse leaned heavily on the arm of the minister. She made a desperate effort to control herself. She clenched her hands until the nails bit into the flesh and bit hard on her lower lip, as she walked slowly down the stairs and into the open where the white-painted gallows stood. Two deputies preceded her and Deputies Ballou and McKinley, who were the executioners, brought up the rear.

Standing on the gallows, Sheriff Cook asked Mrs. Druse if she had anything to say. Looking over the twenty five persons in the courtyard of the jail who had come to watch the spectacle, the woman declined.

Dr. Powell supported Mrs. Druse with one hand while the other he raised high.

"Mrs. Druse desires to ask the forgiveness of all persons whom she may have harmed or injured in any way whatever," the minister said.

As he continued to speak, Mrs. Druse possibly thought of her girlhood in the Town of Marshall, Oneida County and the events leading up to the tragedy.

Forty years before, in 1847, a fairly prosperous farm family named Teft lived in Marshall. Mr. and Mrs. Teft had five children. A little girl, next to the baby was named Roxalana, but was affectionally known as "Roxy."

During the first ten years of her life, Roxy went to school and learned the three R's. She played about her farm home and did chores for her mother.

Her father was taken ill and the farm was mortgaged to meet ever-mounting expenses. Teft, burdened by sickness and worries, died. Mrs. Teft, aided by her two eldest sons, continued to work the farm. The work was too much for the delicate woman. Two years after her husband's passing, Mrs. Teft sickened and died. The children were placed in charge of an uncle.

The uncle allowed the children to continue in school, providing they earned enough money for their clothes.

Roxy grew into womanhood, ambitious and with an education much better than most girls of her day. She was able to converse intelligently and read almost everything she could find. When she was nineteen and attractive, Roxy went to New Hartford to find work as a domestic. While working in the village she attended the Baptist Church.

One day in the fall, a call for hop pickers came from a man residing in the Town of Warren. The farmer was extremely particular. He announced no girl need apply, who was not a member of a church. Roxy Teft and several other New Hartford girls were sent to work. Arrangements were made for them to stay at the home of a minister, the Rev. Northrup.

A young man with a wagon and team met the girls at the railway station. He introduced himself as Bill Druse.

Druse was the son of a well-to-do farmer in the town and was considered a "good catch". He was not considered "wild", but was known to have a churlish and quarrelsome disposition. Druse made his sisters lives so miserable, his father purchased and gave him a hundred-acre farm in the neighborhood, a few miles north of Richfield Springs.

Bill Druse wanted a houskeeper. He began courting Roxy. After the hop picking was over, the girl remained and worked for Rev. and Mrs. Northrup for three years.

Roxy did not love Druse. He always had been kind to her and thoughts of having her own home appealed to her. Against the wishes of her friends, she married him.

The couple had three children, a girl, Mary; a boy, eight years younger, who was named George, and a baby who died in infancy.

Marriage did not change Bill Druse. He grew mean and shiftless. Druse did as little farming as possible. He did not care if his cattle were fed or exposed to rain and snow. He never thought of putting his farm tools under shelter. They lay about the farm, rusting.

Druse neglected his home and buildings. They became weatherbeaten and the roofs leaked.

If he did sow a crop, he was in no hurry to reap it. It was easier to dig a hole in the field and dump his potatoes in than to put them in the cellar of his home. Roxy had to shovel the snow and frozen dirt away in the winter in order to have potatoes for a meal.

If wood for the fire was needed it was easier for him to chop down a nearby apple tree or rip boards from the barn than to hitch up his team and go to the woods. When he was not satisfied with what was on his table, he would go to a neighbor's to eat.

Druse never assumed the blame for anything. He was known to horsewhip his wife and several times had threatened her life. When he swore at Roxy, she swore back.

Druse and Roxy were quarreling at breakfast that morning of December 18, 1884. He went to the barn while Roxy and their daughter, Mary, 18, prepared the frugal meal. When Druse returned he was in ill humor. He started yelling at Roxy for burning up a board he had left near the well. Druse also complained the fire was too hot.

While Druse was at the barn, the family became tired of waiting and had their breakfast. In addition to Mary, there were the Druse's son, George, 10, and Roxy's nephew, Frank Gates, 14.

As Druse sat down to the table he complained a bill he had received from Chet Crim's store near Little Lakes was too high. Part of the bill was for tobacco for himself. He continued his abuse while drinking his tea.

Roxy told her son and nephew to put on their jackets and go out of doors. They went out and a few moments after closing the door, they heard a shot. They rapped to reenter and Mrs. Druse threw open the door. She seemed wild-eyed and excited. Druse was sitting in his chair by the table with blood spurting from a wound in his neck. Mrs. Druse thrust the pistol at Frank Gates; telling him to shoot Druse, or she would shoot him. Frank fired the pistol at his uncle until the chamber was empty. A rope was around Druse's neck and Mary was holding it tightly. Mary dropped the rope and tried to reload the pistol. One cartridge exploded, narrowly missing her.

Duse had fallen from the chair and lay on the floor with his head on the stovehearth. He was still alive. Roxy, who was in a frenzy, seized an old ax near the stove and raised it above her head.

"Oh, Roxy, don't, don't', Druse gasped as the ax descended. Roxy kept chopping away at her husband's head and neck until the head was severed from the body. She wrapped the head in an old newspaper. The boys were sent upstairs to bring down a straw tick. Druse's body was placed on the tick and dragged into the parlor. Roxy closed the parlor doors.

Later in the day, Mrs. Druse came out and sent the boys out for a new ax and for wood and shingles. She kindled fires in both stoves. Frank was sent to fill the boiler with water, which was put on the stove. Roxy then made him clean the blood from the floor, walls and table.

Mary, George and Frank were then told to watch the windows while Mrs. Druse busied herself putting the dismembered parts of her husband into the flames. The dark, meaty-smelling smoke was seen by several neighbors.

Roxy began to let the fires cool down after dark. The next day the ashes were cleaned from the stoves, and placed in a bag. Mrs. Druse, Mary and Frank took the bag with them in a cutter and drove rapidly along the south road to the edge of Wall's swamp. When they were about a quarter of a mile from the Druse home, they buried the ashes under a clump of bushes. Frank kicked snow over the spot. On the way home they tossed the bloody ax and knife, wrapped in old newspapers, into Weatherbee's mill pond.

Druse was missed in his familar haunts. When they inquired where he was, Roxy said he had gone to New York to get a patent on a waterwheel he had invented. The explanation failed to satisfy the neighbors and they continued to ask questions.

On January 6, Roxy went to Richfield Springs and telegraphed her brother, Amon L. Teft in New York City and invited him to come up and bring her husband with him.

The neighbors were still unsatisfied. The Vroomans, Filkins and Petts families, who were near-neighbors of the Druses, remembered seeing the dark, foul-smelling smoke coming from the farmhouse shortly before Druse disappeared.

Knowing of the frequent family quarrels of Mr. and Mrs. Druse, prompted Alonzo Filkins to report his suspicions to the county authorities. On January 9, Fred Vroomen and several other men drove into Richfield Springs to call on Robert Buchanan, the hardware dealer. The men said the ax, wrapped in newspapers, had been found in Weatherbee's pond. Buchanan recognized the ax as one he had sold Druse a short time before.

The excited farmers gathered at a tavern near Little Lakes. Justice of the Peace Daniel McDonald and Clarence Marshall led the investigation.

They got hold of Frank Gates and questioned him until he told of the murder of his uncle. District Attorney Steele of Herkimer County heard the confession and ordered the arrest of Roxalana Druse.

Mrs. Druse, Mary, George, Frank Gates, Charles Gates, who was Roxy's brother-in-law and William Elwood, a neighbor- were arrested.

At the inquest, Charles Gates and Elwood were released after their families proved the men were chopping wood nearly three quarters of a mile away from the Druse home.

At the trial, Roxy was defended by H. Dwight Luce of Richfield Springs, with Judge Prescott as his associate. George Druse was the principal witness against his mother and sister.

Mrs. Druse was found guilty of murder in the first degree and was sentenced to die by hanging. Mary Druse, who was frightened by her mother's sentence, pleaded guilty to murder, second degree. She was sentenced to life imprisonment in Onondaga Penitentiary.

George Druse and Frank Gates were discharged because of their youth. Gates returned to his home in Warren. George was placed under the care of Charles Pett of Warren, who was executor of the Druse estate.

Attorney Luce did not rest. He appealed the death sentence from court to court without success. Luce carried his appeal to

Governor David B. Hill. The Governor twice granted respites. Time was running out for Roxalana Druse.

As the day of execution drew near, Mrs. Druse dictated a statement claiming her daughter, Mary was entirely innocent. She also wrote touching letters to her daughter and son.

At 7 o'clock on that morning of February 28, 1887, Roxy was awakened by the striking of the clock. She proceeded to remove her dress. Instead of wearing the one in which she was to die she put on the black satin she had worn during her trial.

From the street below she could hear the people passing, the men exchanging coarse jokes and the laughter of women. Shortly afterwards the 60-man Remington Rifles took up their posts about the jail.

At 8:10 Roxy received a bouquet of flowers from her daughter. She selected two buds and pinned them on her dress, near her throat.

About 9 o'clock she began to show extreme nervousness.

"Oh, they are going to hang me," she moaned. "What shall I do? I cannot walk to the gallows."

She was finally quieted by the Rev. Powell.

At last Roxy Druse found herself on the gallows. Rev. Powell was finishing his prayer. The executioners pulled her arms behind her and pinioned them. Her ankles were firmly tied and a strap fastened her skirt below her knees. She struggled and moaned but was held firmly. Ballou jerked the black cap over her head and dropped the noose around her neck. Roxy gave another piercing cry before the weight was dropped pulling her into the air. She fell back, her body writhing, until her feet were just above the floor of the gallows. It was just 11:48 in the morning. At 12:14 p.m. she was pronounced dead and the body was taken down.

After a short service the body was taken to Oak Hill Cemetery and interred in a secret spot.

On Sunday, Dr. Powell preached on the subject, "Father, forgive them, for they know not what they do."

BODY IN THE STABLE

It was growing dusk that Friday, March 11, 1856, when Albertus Howard discovered the old horse owned by a neighbor, John Buck, in his barnyard. He asked his son, Franklyn to return the animal.

The rope from the horse's halter trailed under his forefeet and a blanket strapped to his back, was dragging.

Buck lived about a quarter of a mile from the Howard family, on the Third Great Western Turnpike (Route 20), between Morrisville and Nelson. The Buck place was opposite the road from Tinker Hollow (Pleasant Valley) intersected the turnpike.

"Father told me to put the horse into the barn," the youth later recalled. "I went into the house to see if Mr. Buck was there. He was not there and had not been there. Father told me to go up and see what had become of him. I saw him lying on the floor (of the barn). I did not get off the horse, but went back and told my father that I thought he was dead."

Albertus Howard immediately jumped on a horse and went to Buck's barn. It was about 6 p.m.

"(Buck laid with) his head south and his feet north from the door," he said later. "I did not touch him. (I) have known of his falling with fits. After I got off the horse I stepped up to the door and discovered a large gash on the left side of his head."

Howard then went to Issac White's home and met Hiram Blowers and told him Buck was dead. The three returned to Buck's farm, examined the body and discussed what might have happened.

"I saw a deep wound upon his left temple," Howard said. "I then examined the place where we considered he first fell, and saw a large spot of blood. (We) saw his cap lying three feet to the north of this pool of blood. We found upon examination that he was dead. When we came to raise him up, we found two wounds on the back of his head, running from his forehead some four inches."

"When I first saw him my impression was that he might have been injured by a horse, but upon further examination, made up my mind from the nature of the wounds that there had been some foul play . . . . I think it was done with an ax," White remarked.

The men examined Buck's horse and found one if its forefeet was unshod. There was no sign of blood on any of the hooves.

Buck's body was taken to the home of his son-in-law and daughter, Mr. and Mrs. Lonson Clark in Tinker Hollow.

White and some men searched Buck's home and found an ax in the north room. There was blood on the helve. The ax appeared to have been washed. The men also found blood in some of the barnsleepers, six or seven feet above where the body had lain.

Buck was about eighty years of age when he was killed. He was well-known about the countryside. Very little is known of his early years. It was reported he was bound out to a man in one of the eastern states. His master was so cruel, Buck ran away. He reached Whitetown prior to the town meeting in 1800.

From Whitestown he made his way to District 9 in Cazenovia. Buck was about twenty five years old. In addition to the clothing he was wearing, he carried his other possessions in a red bandanna. He also had a pair of heavy cowhide boots and twenty five cents.

As soon as he found a shack in which to live, Buck traded his boots for an ax. He began taking jobs clearing his neighbors lands.

He hoarded the money he earned and at length managed to purchase the eastern part of Lot 14 in District 9 from a man named Lee. He later sold his property to Francis Norton, making a small profit.

Buck then moved to the farm on the turnpike in the eastern part of the Township of Nelson. He put up a cabin and gave shelter to the emigrants moving along the turnpike. Buck also sold drygoods and other merchandise and kept a good stock of liquor and ales. Later he erected a frame house and barn.

He married Sally, whose maiden name is unknown. Mrs. Buck died February 8, 1839 and was buried in the Westcott Cemetery along Tinker Hollow Rd., about a quarter of a mile north of her home.

Buck gave up his tavern business sometime before 1850. He traded his farm produce for things he needed. The day book of Gage and Whitney's Store (now the Nelson Inn) for May 28,

1849, shows Buck was credited for "Butter & Eggs $1.89" and "deduct Tobacco & G. Seeds .31" which left him a balance of $1.58.

It was reported before he was killed, he had sold his farm and was going to spend his remaining days with his relatives.

Circumstantial evidence pointed to George William Zechner, a 26-year old German immigrant, as the murderer. Zechner resided with Myron Mead northwest of the Buck farm.

The suspect was born in Frankfort on-the-Main. He married Mary Bagung of Harburg, Hanover, August 5, 1853. They sailed for the United States from Bremen, November 5, 1853, and arrived in New York on December 20. Their son, Charles, was born October 30, 1855.

Zechner and his family lived with Buck when they came to the area. The immigrant helped with the farm work and clearing a woodlot. Buck frequently told friends Zechner had stolen money from under his pillow.

The German had even visited Buck on the day the old man was killed.

Coroner Sherman of Oneida held an inquest on Saturday, March 22, at the scene and later at the Exchange Hotel in Morrisville. The jury returned their verdict that Buck was murdered and "that the deed was committed with an ax," and that "the testimony taken upon the inquest implicates one George William Zechner as the perpetrator of the murder."

After the jury gave its verdict, Zechner was arrested and committed to the Madison County Jail in Morrisville. He was given an examination before Justice Kern. It began on Wednesday, March 16 and concluded the next day. Zechner was ordered held for action of the Grand Jury.

Zechner was indicted for murder on Tuesday, September 16, and put on trial the following morning before Justice Shankland. David J. Mitchell and Henry C. Goodwin represented the people. The defense was represented by Gerrit Smith of Peterboro, Duane Brown and William H. Kinney.

Smith was convinced of Zechner's innocence and thought the residents were prejudiced, because the immigrant could not speak good English. Smith obtained permission from the New York State Bar to practice law in Zechner's defense.

The jury failed to agree on a verdict the following Saturday morning and was discharged.

Zechner was again put on trial at the adjourned session of the County Oyer and Terminer on Monday, December 1, with Justice Mason presiding. The prosecution and defense counsels remained the same.

The state introduced testimony to show there had been bad feeling between Buck and Zechner. The men had been together about noon the day of Buck's death. It was also pointed out that Zechner was seen on the Buck farm with an ax in his hand.

The motive for the murder was never established. No one witnessed the crime and the evidence was only circumstantial. Smith argued that it was "a murder without a motive, a crime without a cause."

At 10 o'clock Friday morning the jury returned a verdict of "not guilty" and Zechner was released from custody.

Gerrit Smith served Zechner without a fee, and supported his wife and child during his imprisonment. After the immigrant's acquittal, Smith gave him $100 and urged him to stop moving from place to place and to buy a house.

Smith recorded in his diary on Wednesday, January 13, 1858, that Zechner, his wife and two children "left us a few moments ago for Germany". The second child was born after the trial.

On January 19, Smith received a letter from a kinsman that Zechner had reached New York but had disappeared. On the 23rd Smith received word that Zecher was dishonest, quarrelsome, profane; that he chewed tobacco and drank, beat his wife often and threatened to leave her.

In a letter written to the Rev. Samuel May of Syracuse on September 3, 1861, Smith mentioned that Zechner might have killed Buck in an outburst of his uncontrollable temper.

THE TRUMAN FARM

The rambling 125-year old Truman farmhouse squatted on the knoll off the Rose Road, a few miles from the Village of Newport in Herkimer County.

When I last saw it, three decades ago, the building was empty and several of the windows were broken. Glass, paper and rubbish were scattered through the rooms. I wandered slowly through the house that once was filled with the warmth of family living. These rooms had seen and felt laughter and tears, tragedy, births and deaths.

The old, high-backed organ, a total ruin, still stood in its special place against the back wall of the main kitchen. The barren walls and littered floor of the front parlor also brought back memories. From the multi-paned windows I could still see the old pine tree nearby. It still bore the scars of a lightning storm of many years ago. I remember Aunt Libby Truman had been sitting by this window when the lightning bolt struck. It knocked her unconscious and ripped a furrow across the ceiling of the room.

The bedrooms on the second floor evoked no memories of the days long past. I could not recall ever spending a night in any of them. I usually slept in the little room off the big kitchen.

When the Trumans had left their home, they had left a treasure in old spinning wheels and carding machines in the loft. Grandpa Truman's old spice grinder, leaned against the wall, just as he left it.

My memory went back to the early days when the Truman brothers had first settled here.

In the summer of 1798, two weary, footsore brothers stumbled along the deep packed path into Newport. The settlement was composed of a few log cabins clustered on the high ground above West Canada Creek.

They were stopped by a constable who said he was arresting them for traveling on Sunday.

"All right," one brother said, "but I must warn you we think we are coming down with smallpox."

The constable beat a hasty retreat. "Go on," he said, "get out of the area."

Later that day, the brothers stopped at the Bowen cabin and asked if they could spend the night. They gave their names as Daniel and Joseph Truman. The brothers had left their home in Newport, Rhode Island and walked the entire distance to the hamlet of that same name in New York State. They said they were looking for a likely piece of land to settle on.

The next morning, following breakfast, the brothers started in the direction of Norway. Before reaching that settlement, they found a divided path and blazed trees leading off in a northerly direction. They took the blazed trail that led through a swamp and eventually to higher ground some five miles from Newport. What they saw pleased them. Within a few days they purchased twenty five acres of land. They cleared away the trees on the knoll and built a cabin. Enough land was also cleared for planting corn, potatoes and other crops. In the autumn the brothers dug their crops and buried them in a pit as a protection from the cold winter. Daniel and Joseph started on foot to return to their Rhode Island home.

In the spring of 1799, Daniel and Joseph returned to New York State accompanied by three other brothers, John, Thomas and Willian Truman. Daniel's new bride, Nancy Stillman, also came along. She rode on horseback, carrying a few goods for her wilderness home.

The following year, Nancy Truman's parents, Ezra and Polly Newberry Stillman moved, bag and baggage, with their seven children to the settlement. A son, Erastus Stillman, eventually moved to Verona and George Stillman, to Brookfield.

In the shadow of the distant Hasencleaver hills and among the thick evergreens, the Truman brothers made their home. A road was laid out east of the homestead, extending into the Town of Norway. Some of the brothers settled along this road.

Through the years Daniel and Joseph Truman purchased more land until they owned more than 200 acres. In 1802 the frame house was built, a short distance from their log cabin.

Daniel and Nancy Truman had four children, Daniel Jr., Sally, Oliver Hazard Perry and John. Nancy Truman died in 1835. Daniel afterwards married Desire Burdick of Brookfield in Madison County.

Oliver Hazard Perry and his wife, Lydia Knight, were the next owners of the homestead. It passed from them to their son, Alexander Truman. Alexander was born in 1836. In his later years he was known to all, with great affection, as "Grandpa" Truman.

Grandpa Truman was a link between the pioneer days and the present. His days of hard work were over. His shoulders were bent with age and hard work; his hair and beard were white as the snow of winter. His eyes were always gentle.

He remembered when wild animals roamed close to the house. Food was raised on the farm as well as the wool from which the family clothes were made.

"Grandpa (Daniel) always tried to keep a fire going at night to keep the animals away," he said. "Grandpa woke up one night to find the fire out and the baby, Sally, missing from her crib. He was afraid the baby had crawled from the cabin and the bears had got her.

"When daylight came the baby was found on two logs near the fireplace fast asleep. Live coals had to be carried from the Stillman place half a mile away to get the fire started again," he remembered.

When Alexander Truman was about twenty four years of age he started courting Jane Coombs, who lived up the road about half a mile. His hound dog always followed him. One night when Truman started for home, he could not find his dog. As he walked along in the darkness, Alexander heard the the sound of padded feet following him. Truman started to run and the padded feet also seemed to speed up. Coming to a rail fence, Alexander quickly climbed over it as the animal leaped. Down went Truman into the ditch. He could feel a hot breath on his face. He tried to yell, but no sound came from him. He threshed wildly and finally dislodged the animal. He managed to catch a glimpse of the animal . . . . it was his faithful hound.

Grandpa used to laugh when he told the story. He said it was no laughing matter at the time. He remembered panthers following him sometimes when he was hunting.

Truman and Jane Coombs were married on January 30, 1860. They had a son, Charles I. Truman. Charles grew up and married Libby Bennet, whose family lived in Gray. The couple had two children, Orville and Bessie Truman. This is mentioned, because Grandpa's life was closely interwoven with his family.

Grandpa was a prognosticator. Every morning and afternoon in good or bad weather, he would go out the back door and stare at the cloud formations. When he reentered the house, he would say casually, "It's going to be a nice day tomorrow, so we can get the hay in," or, "You'd best get all the work you can done today. It is going to rain hard tomorrow."

His predictions were always infallable. Grandpa Truman had been dead more than twenty years before Bessie Truman said the old man studied astronomy and meterology at Fairfield Academy in nearby Fairfield. He had many books on the subject.

Grandpa was also gifted with second sight. One morning he arose about daylight and walked to the spring house to draw a pail of water. As he turned to leave he saw a gray-haired woman coming to the spring. She called him by name. When she drew nearer he saw it was a neighbor, Aunt Sally Root, who was about ninety years of age.

"Why, Auntie, what are you doing here?" he asked.

Aunt Sally failed to answer. When he looked again, the old lady had disappeared.

Alexander said nothing to his family, afraid they would laugh at him. Later that day, Aunt Sally's grandson, Elmer Ives drove down from back of Norway to say the old lady had died that morning. Grandpa Truman and Ives compared the time. Aunt Sally had died about the time Grandpa had seen her at the well.

The farm north of the Truman's was owned, in 1910, by Thomas Spring. One wintery night the family was sitting in their warm kitchen. Grandpa suddenly lifted his head, listening.

"There's someone at the door," he said. Charlie, Libby and the children listened, but heard nothing.

"Someone's stomping on the porch," Grandpa said. "Can't you hear him? "Can't you hear him cleaning the snow from his boots. Sounds like Tom Spring."

Libby went to the door and opened it. There was no one there. "See, you are wrong, father," she remarked.

Grandpa Truman shook his head sadly. "Well, old Tom is dead. Guess he stopped by to say good bye,"

The next morning, Bill Spring one of Tom's sons, stopped by to inform the family his father had died the night before.

An old cord clork was one of the Truman heirlooms. Like many other pieces of the antique furnishings, it "disappeared" after the farm was sold in the early 1930's. The clock had no springs, weights or string to operate it. It had been in the house's loft about seventy five years, silent. When Grandpa

Truman's mother, Lydia Truman, died, the clock suddenly came to life and struck the day, month and hour.

The clock was silent again until that day in 1912 when Grandma Jane Coombs, Grandpa's wife, died. Seconds before she died, the clock became awake and struck thirteen times.

Grandma Rebecca Bennet and I were at the Truman farm in 1915 when Orville came home from the milk station one morning, flushed with excitement.

"There's a big band of Gypies camped on the Poland Road," he said. "They will be coming this way. We will have to watch them or they will steal everything in sight."

A few day later two of the Gypsy wagons, brightly decorated as if for a carnival, and pulled by splendid teams, drove into the yard. Aunt Libby, Grandma Bennet and I hid while Grandpa Truman and Orville went to the door to speak to the Gypsies. I don't know the words that were exchanged, but shortly afterwards the men and the wagons left. Orville said he wouldn't feel right until the caravan left the Poland Road.

A few year's later, the family had its first horseless carriage. Orville purchased the car, which looked like a converted carriage with hard tires, from a Newport doctor.

Orville had quite a time learning to drive. The contraption started for the barn one day and Orville forgot how to stop it. He pulled hard on the steering wheel, hollering, "Whoa, whoa, damn you — stop!"

The steering wheel came off and the car stopped, when it hit the side of the barn.

One by one the older folks passed away until only Orville and Bessie were left. The farm was sold and for the first time in more than 125 years, the house was empty.

The house, seemed broken and forlorn, after so many years of family warmth. It stood on the knoll when I last saw it in the early 1930's . . . . . I never have been back.

THE BODY SNATCHERS

The body of Harry Burrell of Little Falls was taken from the vault in the Church Street Cemetery in Little Falls on the night of April 21, 1879 for the purpose of holding it for ransom.

Mr. Burrell, who had died about eight weeks previously, was a "merchant prince" of the village and considered one of its wealthiest men.

This is the story of the happening:

About 7:30 Tuesday morning, April 22, David Becker and James Powers found the receiving vault in the cemetery had been entered and the body of Mr. Burrell's taken.

The men had gone to the vault to remove the body of Richard Searles for reinternment. They found the padlock fastening the iron bar that protected the front doors of the vault had been pried open. Entering, they walked down the inside stone steps to the inner doors. They found them opened sufficiently to permit entrance. The iron bar across them was bent.

In the inner vault they found the cover on a rough box holding the body of a girl had been removed and replaced. The box containing the body of Mr. Burrell was open and the empty casket lay on the floor. The slippers worn by the corpse, and the droppings from a candle were in the casket. A lock of hair was found near the door. The body had been taken.

Becker went immediately to the Burrell mansion and notified David Burrell his father's body was missing. News of the theft of the body spread rapidly through the village. The police immediately placed residents along the Mohawk River banks and on the roads leading from the village to search for the body.

Some residents reported hearing a horse and wagon traveling at a rapid pace on Monroe Street about midnight. Thomas Fox, who resided across the river, reported his horse and wagon had been taken from his barn about 10 o'clock the previous evening and returned before morning. He said his horse was in an exhausted condition from hard driving. The course of the wagon was easily traced by the marks left by a wobbly rear wheel. The police followed the wagon tracks along the towpath of the canal to Finck's bridge, to the residence of D. Hess at Fall Hill, then back to the Fox home. The searching party were confused. It was reported Hess's chicken coop had been burglarized and the wagon was used to carry the chickens away.

The police found a sack of tobacco and a lock of hair in the wagon. The hair matched a lock that had caught on the inner door of the cemetery vault.

The investigators theorized the body snatchers had driven to Finck's Basin, crossed the bridge and came up the north side to reach the cemetery by way of the back streets. After removing the body, they returned the same way. In this way, they avoided meeting the police.

After the body snatchers reached the Basin again, the tracks appeared to travel over Fall Hill to reach the south side of the village. The men drove through the streets until they came to the bridge over the canal near P.C. Casler's barn. They crossed over the bridge and continued until they reached the spot where they concealed the body. The thieves returned the horse and wagon to the Fox home. The driving was to baffle seachers.

Aroused citizens met in the Hook and Ladder Company rooms and armed patrols formed to guard all roads leading from the city.

A few days later Rodney House, while searching for eggs, heard chickens cackling under his brother's barn at nearby Jacksonburgh. House found a hole about five feet from the bottom of the stone wall under the barn. He crawled through and had traveled about twenty-five feet when he came to a large oblong bundle wrapped in an old blanket and piece of sacking. House pulled a corner of the blanket away and discovered it was the body of a man.

He immediately notified his brother, Squire House. The brothers examined the body and decided it was that of Mr. Burrell. They drove to Little Falls and notified David Burrell. Burrell and James Churchill returned with the brothers. Burrell identified the remains as those of his father. He and Churchill placed the body in a closed carriage and drove to the Undertaking Parlors of H. A. Tozer and Company.

The necktie on the deceased had been removed and used to tie the arms. The ankles were also tied to make transportation easier.

About the time the body was recovered, Officer Charles Shepardson arrested 23-year old Thomas "Happy Jack" Kane on a charge of stealing the body. Because of the explosive temper of the residents, Kane was taken to the Herkimer County Jail. He was returned next morning by Officer Shepardson and arraigned before Justice Smith. Kane waived examination to the charge and was ordered held for action of the Grand Jury. In lieu of $2,000 bail, he was committed to the jail.

A few days later, William Gross, was arrested on the same charge. He also waived examination to the charge and was ordered held for grand jury action. He was also committed to the county jail when he was unable to post $1,000 bail. Gross was later exonerated of any part of the crime and released.

While in jail, "Happy Jack" Kane told the entire story of the theft of Mr. Burrell's body to Detective Wheeler of the local Police Department. He blamed William Keating, a 22-year old man from Oneida, whom he knew as "William Van Alstyne" as the leader. Kane also "fingered" VanAlstyne for the burglary of the home of Mr. and Mrs. Alvin Richmond, sometime before the theft of the body.

Kane said the body snatching was discussed about 9 o'clock Friday night, April 18 by VanAlstyne while they were on the bridge near John Shoemaker's place in Little Falls. VanAlstyne said they could remove the body of Mr. Burrell from the vault and hide it, Kane said. VanAlstyne estimated the Burrell family would willingly pay $15,000 or $20,000 for the recovery. The Oneidan said he thought he could get Newton "Pop" Lewis of Jacksonburgh to help.

Happy Jack said the job was planned for Monday night, April 21. VanAlstyne said he would need a candle. He could get a crowbar. Pop Lewis agreed to help the two men. While Lewis would not take part in stealing the body, he would find a place where it could be hidden.

Van Alstyne and Kane stole Fox's horse and wagon that Monday night and drove from Finck's Basin up the Erie Canal about two miles. After passing through Manheim, they returned to Little Falls about 10:30. They left the horse and wagon in the cemetery and removed the blanket and sacking, the crowbar and candle and walked to the vault.

VanAlstyne pried open the outer lock and the men entered the vault. They closed the doors and Kane lighted the candle. They walked down the stone steps and pried on the doors leading to the inner vault. The bar holding the doors, was bent enough to allow the doors to be pushed open enough to allow them to crawl through.

Kane said they took the cover off a rough box and seeing the name of a girl on the coffin, replaced the lid, but did not replace the screws. The next box they opened happened to be that of Mr. Burrell. They removed the coffin, opened it and removed the body.

The candle Happy Jack was holding dropped some of its grease on the coffin. As he attempted to snuff the wick, the light went out. As neither man had another match, they left. VanAlstyne drove down Main Street and let Kane out to get some matches. When Happy Jack returned, VanAlstyne drove back to the cemetery. They re-entered the vault and brought out Mr. Burrell's body. Having wrapped it, the men placed it in the wagon and drove off as rapidly as the horse could go. It was about 2:30 in the morning when they went down Church Street.

Van Alstyne left the wagon near the foot of the hill and soon returned with Pop Lewis. "Have you got him?" Pop asked. "Yes," Happy Jack replied.

"Well, let's get this thing done up and get away before anyone sees us," Lewis said. He went to get a board.

The body was taken to the House farm and by using the board, the men managed to hide the body under the barn. They returned to the Fox place to leave the horse and wagon before going to their own homes.

Kane said he met VanAlstyne the next day, but pretended not to know him.

The Herkimer County Grand Jury found indictments against the three men on the following Tuesday. Keating, alias VanAlstyne was also indicted for burglarizing the Richmond home.

Happy Jack and Pop Lewis were arraigned separately and pleaded guilty to the indictment. VanAlstyne pleaded innocent to the indictments and demanded a trial. District Attorney Duddleston moved for VanAlstyne's trial on the burglary charge first.

VanAlstyne said he expected to be defended by Attorney P. H. McAvoy and a constable from "back home" (Oneida). When the trial began he was represented by Attorneys McAvoy and George W. Smith. Judge Amos H. Prescott presided with H. P. Kibbie and C. P. Miller as associate justices.

Kane testified against VanAlstyne. He admitted frankly he was an informer.

VanAlstyne was found guilty of the burglary by the jury on the following afternoon. The trial for stealing the body of Mr. Burrell immediately started. Van Alstyne was also found guilty of this charge.

Brought before the court, Van Alstyne said he was not the leader of the "gang" as had been charged. He said there were others in on the body stealing. VanAlstyne also complained of Happy Jack and Lewis "squealing".

Judge Prescott replied that society must be protected He sentenced VanAlstyne to ten years in Auburn State Prison on the burglary charge and to five years for the body stealing.

Happy Jack Kane was given five years in Auburn Prison. Judge Prescott said he would not sentence him for his part in the Richmond burglary. Lewis was also sentenced to five years.

MR. COLGATE

In 1890, James D. Colgate of New York City gave a quarter of a million dollars to Madison University in Hamilton. The money was just enough to build a library.

The Board of Trustees decided to honor the benefactor by renaming the university in his honor. In March, 1891, Colgate notified the university he was coming to Hamilton. The professors, 134 college students and 100 students in the preparatory school planned a grand reception.

On the day Mr. Colgate was scheduled to arrive, the students rented a hack from Felton's Livery Stable that stood in the rear of the Park House, decorated it and tied a rope, so they could pull it. The students and professors took the hack and went to the New York, Ontario and Western Railway Station to wait the arrival of the train.

The train from the north finally pulled into the station. No one had seen Mr. Colgate, but the welcoming crowd had a good description. "There he is," someone shouted as a dignified gray-haired gentlemen stepped from the train. The students quickly escorted the gentleman to the hack and helped him in, piling his satchels in the rear. Singing and shouting praises for the benefactor of the university, the students pulled the hack down Lebanon Street to the Park House. No one could have felt more honored by the welcome.

Upon arriving at the hotel, the dignified man in the hack climbed down and shook hands with the students, professors and townspeople.

"Well, I've traveled all my life, and never had such a welcome," he exclaimed. "I'm Jerry Taylor, a whiskey and cigar salesman. Come on in —" he indicated the Park House, "and have a drink."

Some of those who attended, said the party lasted for hours.

RENDEZVOUS AT NORWICH

On the 18th of June, 1812, President James Madison, who was known for his peace feelings, laid his war message before Congress. It was acted upon the same day. The United States was again at war with Great Britian.

The thirst for war pervaded the Chenango Valley. Many of the residents were descendants of the men of 1776. They waited the call to arms.

On September 8, 400 volunteers and draftees rendezvoused at Norwich. A sea of white tents lay among the big pine stumps not far from Moses Doty's Hotel.

About half the regiment was composed of Chenango County men. The remainder was made up from Broome and Tioga Counties.

The men picked their own officers to lead them. They were: Lieutenant Colonel Thompson Meade, of Norwich, as commandant; Major John Randall Jr., Norwich; Judge John Noyes Sr., adjutant; Asa Norton, of the same place, quartermaster; Dr. William Mason of Preston, was surgeon; Reuben Gray, Sherburne; Nathan Taylor, South New Berlin; Thorton Wasson, Guilford and Daniel Root, Pitcher, all as captains; Charles Randall of Captain Gray's Company and John Fields, who had formerly been a British officer, as lieutenants. A man named Clark was made the second major. Solomon Smith and a man named Williams were selected as captains for the soldiers from Broome County.

Lieut. Col. Mead received his orders and September 20, the regiment broke camp and started for the northern frontier. Led by the music of fifes and drums, the regiment spread out for nearly a mile.

The line of march led through Sherburne, Log City, Cazenovia, Onondaga, Cayuga Bridge, Canandaigua and Batavia. The regiment arrived in Buffalo early in October. Part of the way they marched with men from Colonel Stranahan's regiment.

The day after their arrival they marched down the Niagara River and took up positions on the American side of the river opposite Queenstown Heights.

A massing of boats on the American side was seen during a heavy rain storm that swept the frontier on October 12th. General Issac Brock, the lieutenant governor of Upper Canada was told. He said it would be a good time for an attack, but did not think the Americans would.

At dawn on the following morning, while it was still storming, 100 members of Mead's regiment took to the boats and were rowed across the St. Lawrence River to Queenstown Heights. Lt. Col. Mead, Captain Bacon, Wasson and Root and Lieutenants Randall and Fields were with their men. They met Colonel Solomon VanRensselaer returning in a boat with his badly wounded.

The soldiers and officers landed without incident and joined the other troops before ascending the hill. When they reached the top, they took their positions in the open field, about thirty rods from where a line of Indians lay secreted behind the trees and a heavy rail fence.

The Indians poured a deadly fire into the regiments. Mead was fired upon continuously as he walked to and fro, giving orders. Sergeant Mann was shot while at his commander's side. Realizing the danger of their exposed position, Lieutenant Randall led a charge. It succeeded in putting the Indians to flight.

In the meantime, the invasion of Canada had gone on. All boats that could be collected were employed to transport Lt. Col. Christie and VanRensselaer's troops across the river. Unfortunately there were too few boats to transport large numbers. By this time the invading Americans were under heavy British fire.

Colonel VanRenselaer landed, but before he could form his men, he was wounded in several places. About the same time nearly every officer and non-commissioned officer who was crossing the river was either killed or wounded by the fire. A whole boatload of Americans was struck by grape-shot and killed. The water was soon covered by wounded or the dead.

Although wounded, VanRensselaer ordered the men to mount the hill and silence the British battery. Captain Wool and others promptly obeyed, carried the position, and routed the enemy.

The retreating British and Canadians were rallied by General Brock. It was his last act. He was leading the charge

97

when he was shot below the heart by an American sharp-shooter.

The British troops were again repulsed, but the rest was short. British soldiers at Fort George, only eight miles away, had heard the firing, and were on the way. More than 500 Indians joined them.

Faced now by 1,300 men, the Americans were forced back. There were no boats on the Canadian side for them to recross the river. The militia with the boats on the American side refused to come to their aid. Colonel Winfield Scott mounted a log in front of the men.

"The enemies balls begin to thin our ranks," he said. "His numbers are overwhelming. In a moment the shock must come and there is no retreat. We are in the beginning of a national war. Hull's surrender must be redeemed. Let us die, arms in hand. Our country demands the sacrifice. The blood of the slain will make heroes of the living. Those who follow will avenge our fall and their country's wrongs.

"Who dare to stand?" he asked. "All" the men shouted.

The British under the command of General Sheaffe, maneuvered with great caution. Although thrown back several times, they finally forced Scott to surrender.

About 100 were killed, 200 captured and the remainder of about 300 surrendered with Scott. The prisoners, including Colonel Mead's regiment were taken to Niagara and later to Newark.

Lieut. Randall was greatly admired by his captors for his courage. Lieut. Fields fell into the hands of his former British commander, but escaped recognition. If he had been identified, he would have been shot as a traitor.

Parole was granted the prisoners on October 19, and they returned to their homes. The survivors of the Chenango regiment returned to Norwich.

THE LEGEND OF OWAHGENA LAKE

Long before the coming of the white man, Owahgena Lake, the Lake of the Yellow Perch (better known as Cazenovia Lake), was the dividing line between the Onondagas and Oneidas.

In those days before the Iroquois Confederacy, the Oneidas had a village on what later became known as the Krumbhaar Estate, north of the Village of Cazenovia. The Onondaga Village was located near present Oran. While the two villages were not at war, each regarded the other with suspicion.

One spring morning a party of Onondagas returned and said the Oneidas had broken the treaty and were fishing in the Onondaga's side of the lake. A pow-wow followed. Instead of attacking the Oneidas, the wiser chiefs decided to send Natoka, a young brave and son of Chief Nagua to confer with the Oneida chiefs on the violation.

The Oneidas listened solemly to Natoka in their long house and smoked a pipe of peace. As Natoka was leaving he saw Malaka, the daughter of Chief Tewansah of the Oneidas. The pretty young woman showed interest in the Onondaga warrior with a glance from her dark eyes.

During the following week, Natoka found excuses to visit the Oneida village under the guise of reopening the negotiations of the use of the lake. Actually he wanted to see Malaka. Natoka, finding the maiden returned his love, went to her father and asked what he might want for his daughter. Chief Tewansah listened and then told Natoka that as long as the moon journeyed across the heavens, his daughter would never dwell in the land of the Onondagas. The chief ordered the brave to leave his village.

During the summer when Malaka heard the sound of an owl's hoot from an alder grove near the Brook of Shadows, she would leave her father's house and silently steal through the woods to meet her lover. The young Onondaga brave tried to persuade her to go with him. She refused, saying she did not wish to oppose her father's will. An Oneida warrior had already asked her father to take her as his wife.

Natoka finally decided strong measures were necessary. Accompanied by five friends, the brave crossed the lake one dark night to the Oneida side. Silently the Onondagas went from canoe to canoe of the Oneidas, cutting the deer thongs binding the sides. Natoka then gave the owl's hoot.

When Malaka stole from her house to join him, the Onondagas seized her. Placing her in one of their canoes, they paddled furously across the lake.

The Oneida brave, who also sought Malaka, witnessed her kidnapping and spread the alarm. The brave and Chief Tewansah and other warriors discovered their damaged canoes. However there was one the Onondagas had missed. It was quickly launched by Chief Tewansah and some of his warriors. The Chief's canoe gained rapidly.

Near the Shadow of the Pines on the opposite side of the lake, Natoka placed an arrow to his bow and let fly. The arrow struck the side of the Oneida's canoe, causing it to overturn and spill its occupants into the water.

The warriors rescued Chief Tewansah, but Natoka and his party escaped, carrying Malaka with them. A few days later the lovers were married and started on a trip to the western lands of the Senecas.

Chief Tewansah never recovered from his emersion in the cold waters of the lake. As it became apparent he would soon make the long journey to the Happy Hunting Ground, he expressed a desire to see his daughter once more.

Natoka and Malaka were finally located on the shores of Cayuga Lake. They immediately started homeward. Late on the third day they reached the Onondaga village, but were too fatigued to continue.

That night, knowing the end was near, Chief Tewansah summoned his warriors. He requested his body be placed in a canoe and sunk in the lake near the Shadows of the Pines where he had last seen his daughter.

The Chief's spirit fled before the morning sun arose. As Natoka and Malaka were starting on their journey to visit her father, the warriors of the Oneida Nation towed the canoe containing the body of Chief Tewansah to the Shadow of the Pines. Filling the canoe with rocks, it finally sank beneath the water of the Lake of the Yellow Perch.

THE CANOE

An old Indian canoe was recovered near the Shadow of the Pines (Beckwith Bay) on Owahgena Lake at Cazenovia in the summer of 1860 by a group of young divers.

It was near the scene where, according to Oneida and Onondaga Indian legends, the canoe containing the body of Chief Tewansah of the Oneidas, was sunk, long before the coming of the white man.

The canoe was found, filled with stones, on the bottom of the lake. No human bones were in the canoe.

At the time, the Cazenovia Republican, said, "The closest inspection failed to see any indication of youth about it, and its two or three wrought nails and scraps of iron might well have been bought with beaver skins at the Jesuit settlements in Onondaga about 1650 or 1670. Its antiquity was considered to be satisfactorily established and all agreed to believe it."

As soon as the Onondaga Indians at Nedrow heard of the canoe being brought to shore, they launched a vigorous protest. The youth, who recovered the canoe, decided to sink it again.

A program was arranged by residents of Cazenovia to make the ceremony part of a water festival.

Two photographs were taken by E. C. Covell of Cazenovia. One of them shows the large canoe floating near the shore with three men in it. They were identified as Richard Parsons, Ebenezer Knowlton and John Fairchild. The other, taken on Saturday, October 12, 1861, after the sinking of the canoe, is of a group of residents dressed in Indian costume.

At one o'clock on that afternoon, the pier on the lake was crowded with spectators. The boats began to gather around the old canoe, which was floating on the lake, "which looked ancient enough to have belonged to the very first Indian who ever paddled," the Republican reported.

Many of the rowboats were decorated with bright flags and the oars were manned by young men wearing red jackets. There were also sailboats and flat-bottomed boats, each with "Indian warriors" and "squaws" in costume.

"While waiting the arrival of the braves, the merry assemblage occupied themselves with mutual admiration and watched the sailboats," the Cazenovia Republican said. "Of these the Imp was most active, dashing up to the pier and wheeling away half on edge, like a dexterous skater, while the stately Acandecca (Daughter of the Snows) under the skillful seamanship of Kanyatera (Salt Water) cleft the waves like a frigate, and Flying Cloud, sailed by Onikanos (Fresh Water) veered and wheeled like a white seagull. The Chief, a large flat-bottomed boat, belonging to Rokawano (Master of Canoes) made a fine appearance and carried twenty three persons in safety."

The "Indian warriors" appeared upon the scene at two o'clock and were marshalled on the shore by the six-foot War Chief Natongura (Black Eagle). Among them were Shaw-Shaw (Swallow), his 17-year old bride and Nokoms, the chief's grandmother, a stout matron, but a person of great importance.

Embarking in the boats and canoes and forming a guard of honor around the old canoe, the "Indians" sailed across the lake to the Shadow of Pines (Beckwith Bay). The warrior and his bride were welcomed to shore. A council fire was built and the "warriors" expressed their hospitality by dancing.

Chief Medo-Howa (He Who Knows the Laws) stepped forward and raising his right arm, addressed the "braves"; "Brothers! The tribes have assembled today to perform the sacred duty of restoring to its final resting place the ancient canoe, the sight which has revived so many traditions of the past."

The Chief went on to say it was fitting that the canoe, a relic of the past, which once sped across the lake, should again be restored to its bed beneath the waters.

"Brothers! It is a subject of congratulations that you have been enabled with so little preparation to reproduce with fidelity and effect these solemn rites and ceremonies with which the red men were wont to celebrate an occasion like this," Chief Medo-Howa said. "At the return of each harvest let us, year by year, with our women and little ones, assemble upon these lovely waters and with varying pomp and solemn ceremonial, gather up some of the traditions of the past and enjoy the present and to the full, the natural advantages of scenery which the Great Spirit has given for our enjoyment."

Along the shore, the ceremony was about to start. Kokonoki (He Who Keeps the Time) and several other "braves" raised the old canoe, filling it with stones. Although the waves on the lake were high, the canoe slid quickly to the bottom, its last resting place. The "warriors" raised a parting cry.

The celebration was over and the "Indians" started for home as the sky darkened and a storm threatened.

THE CHAUTAUQUA

The big, brown tents of the Redpath Chautauqua were a familiar sight for many years in many communities as Oneida, Cazenovia, Hamilton, Norwich and others, extending from Niagara Falls to Maine.

George I. Bennett of Glen Rock, N. J., formerly of Hamilton, who traveled the Chautauqua circuit during the earlier days, estimated that in the peak year, 1924, more than 30 million Americans in some 12 thousand villages and cities enjoyed the lectures, concerts, plays and other features during a typical week.

"The tent Chautauqua was a typical American institution." Bennett said. "As one speaker put it, humorously, 'America is noted for three things, ice cream, corn-on-the-cob and Chautauqua!' Another declared, 'Homespun and heart warming, Chautauqua was as American as corn-pone and just as body-building.' "

"The changing times, airplanes, movies and radio put an end to the tent Chautauqua," Bennett added.

He recalled many events, humorous and almost tragic that occurred during those days of travel.

One week, Chautauqua Tent No. 8 was in Oneida. On this particular night Victor Herbert's operetta, "The Fortune Teller" was on the program. A large audience was in the tent. The time came for the orchestra to start the opening strains of the overture, when it was discovered one of the principal members of the cast was missing. He was Eddie   , one of the two comedians.

A search was made backstage. Neither the cast or crew had seen him for some hours and no one knew where he was. After a hurried consultation, two of the crew boys were sent to the hotel where the local directory, pinned up in the wings, indicated was his lodging place.

Eddy was found, asleep in bed. He had apparently become completely exhausted by the strain of the nightly appearances in the operetta, traveling as well as his special daily task. This task was to hunt up people whom he could work into his routine.

The crew boys dragged Eddy from bed, dashed cold water into his face, managed to get him dressed, and then pulled him to the tent and got him into his costume.

"All this took time," Bennett said. "The hour for the opening of the show had passed. The audience was getting restless. Some began rhythmic hand-clapping. It was almost nine o'clock before the curtain rose on the first act.

"The cast and crew faced an ordeal. No one knew how the audience would react. Like all Herbert's musical shows, "The Fortune Teller' was light opera and very popular. Some members of the audience had helped underwrite the production. If the audience did not like it, they would make their feelings known. If they approved, their applause would tell. The answer to the speculation came before the end of the first act," Bennet said.

"Eddie and Dutch, the two comedians, were introducing one of their specialities, a topical song, which gave them the opportunity to bring in the names of local persons and places — always a sure-fire laugh.

"Eddy would sing a clever line, ending, 'Do you follow me?' to which Dutch would chime in, 'I certainly do!'," Bennett recalled.

"A few bars of music by the orchestra was the signal for Eddie to begin," Bennett said. "His opening words brought the laugh of the evening. Turning to Dutch, Eddie said, 'Sound your A.' Just as Dutch responded, Oneida's nine o'clock alarm whistle and time signal boomed out loud and clear over the city."

"If it had been planned, the effect could not have been more perfect," The pitch of the whistle was exactly that of Dutch as he sounded his A. It was like a long, loud extension of the comedian's voice. The effect was instantaneous. A great roar of laughter and applause swept over the audience. Some were almost in hysterics.

"Eddie realized what had happened and what an opportunity it was giving him to get in an extra joke," Bennett said. "He knew what to do for he was an experienced trouper. Some time was lost waiting for silence. He stood his ground and waited. When the laughter and applause finally died down, Eddy said, "Dutch. I've been doing this act with you for a long time and this is the first time you sounded your A on absolutely the right tone and pitch.' "

"This brought another gale of laughter," Bennett said. "It was sometime before quiet was restored and the show could go on. It was the high spot of the performance. The cast caught the enthusiasm and spontaneity the comedians had generated. This quickly infected the audience.

"Later that evening Eddie was greeted with warm applause when he gave a fine rendition of the song, which includes the lilting melody, 'Slumber on, my little gypsy sweetheart.'

"The show sparkled that night and scintillated from the first note of the overture to the last strains of the finale," Bennett said. "Long afterwards, it was remembered the cooperation of Oneida's nine o'clock whistle when Eddie commanded, 'Sound your A.' "

The Chautauqua also introduced many reknown speakers to rural America. Bennett recalled one of these as the Honorable J. Hugh Edwards, Welsh statesman and a member of the British Parliment. He was a member of the British Liberal Party, a staunch supporter and close friend of the Prime Minister David Lloyd George.

"The honorable Mr. Edwards always had his traditional "spot of tea" in the afternoon. He was very successful on the circuit," Bennett said. "In later years he wrote the definite biography of David Lloyd George and became a distinguished member of "The Authors Club."

There were a few times when danger threatened the Chautauqua. One such incident occurred one June morning in the late 1920's after the show had left the Village of Ransomville in Niagara County, on a division of the New York Central Railroad.

Bennett said the boys had worked all night taking down the tent and had completed loading it by daybreak. When the work was completed, the boys went for a swim, had their breakfast and soon were asleep in their car.

"We arrived at the railroad station of the Suspension Bridge after a short run," Bennett recalled. "Here our car was to be shifted to another train to continue our trip to our next stop in Western New York. The car was standing directly in front of the depot. A small crowd of passengers were seated on benches and standing on the platform waiting for the train to be made up."

"The track on which our baggage car was standing ran west, down a long slope toward a large level area beyond which was the gorge of the Niagara River. At the foot of the hill the track merged with a network of tracks with many signal towers, semaphores, crossings and switches. Here engines were moving cars back and forth.

"Suddenly," Bennett said, "we heard cries of alarm. A worker in the railroad yard noticed the brakes on our car had not been set tight enough to hold it. The brakes had loosened and the car was in motion, first rolling slowly, but soon picking up speed as it sped down the slope toward disaster."

"Luckily the yard engine was behind our car," Bennett said, "and on the same track. When the engineer's attention was drawn toward our car by the cries, he sprang into motion. He pulled open his throttle and gave quick chase after the runaway car.

"Meanwhile the fireman climbed out of the cab and worked his way slowly along the side of the locomotive and climbed onto the cowcatcher. Here he waited coupling in hand. The engine quickly overtook the run-a-way car and bumped into it with a resounding whack. The fireman dropped the coupling connecting the engine with the car. The engineer applied his brakes and the car was stopped with a tremendous jolt.

"The sudden jolting of the train practically threw the sleeping boys out of their bunks in the car," Bennett said. They opened the sliding door and looked out. The dazed and wondering expressions on their faces brought laughter and cheers from the small crowd. The scare was over," Bennett said. "Soon our train was made up and we were jogging along to the next town on our itinerary.

THE EARL GANG

Mrs. Chloe Ann Moon refused to be quiet that summer night in the 1880's after the burglar tried to chloroform her. Her yells caused him to flee. In a way she was indirectly responsible for the downfall of the Earl Gang.

The gang which had its headquarters on Franklin Street in Syracuse was composed of Leon Earl, the leader; his brother, Charles and Charles's wife, Emma; James Bryan, Tom Jacques and Frank Rivers, who was also known as Rickard.

For several years, the gang, like the Loomis Gang of Sangerfield, terrorized the cities and countryside in Upstate New York. There was no connection between the gangs.

The major part of the Earl Gang's thefts were fenced in Cooperstown, Michigan, by a brother-in-law of the leader.

Their undoing was laid to the burglaries of the homes of Dr. T. H. French of Chittenango; Stephen Goff and Abram Moon of Merrillsville.

Rivers was known as a "Crick" boy as he worked on various farms along the Cowaselone Creek in the valley. Like all the neighbors he knew the Goff and Moon families were prominent farmers and possessed property of value. Rivers worked for Moon for three seasons, including just before the burglary. He knew where the silverware was kept as well as Moon's prized possession, his gold watch. The farmer kept it in a collar box beside his bed. Rivers also knew Moon planned to have a large sum of money in the house.

Moon had drawn nearly $300 from an Oneida bank that day to pay a debt. It started to rain that night and Moon saw it was unusually dark outside.

"Most anything could happen on a night like this," he told his wife. He removed his wallet containing the money from his pocket and tossed it under the six-legged, drop leaf table in the sitting room. A short time later he and Chloe Ann went to bed.

Rivers had planned the burglaries of homes in the valley a few months before. He met Jacques during hop picking time the previous fall. They sat on East Hill overlooking the valley. Rivers pointed out the location of the Goff and Moon farms.

On the night selected, Rivers and Jacques drove down the Merrillsville Road. They went up Stockbridge East Hill and entered the Goff home. Using chloroform, they soon had Stephen Goff unconscious. They removed $67 from the farmer's pocket and left. Rivers and Jacques started for the Moon home.

Reaching the home, they quietly forced an entrance. Posting Jacques by the floor-length window in the sitting room overlooking the road, Rivers poured some chloroform onto a wad of cloth. Walking lightly into the Moon's bedroom, he lay the saturated cloth on Abram's face. While Moon was slipping into deep slumber. Rivers removed the farmer's gold watch from its box near the bed. Rivers then returned to the sitting room and entered the pantry off the kitchen. Picking up the Moon's best silverware, he returned to the sitting room and handed it to Jacques. Rivers went into the bedroom again and placed the chloroform soaked rag over Chloe Ann's face. He was starting to paw through the dresser drawers, when the woman awakened.

Although Rivers was masked, it did not deter Chloe Ann. "What do you want?" she shouted. "What are you doing here?"

Rivers tried to calm her, but it did not work. He tried threatening her. It did not work either.

Chloe Ann, who was described by her grandson, Carl Moon of Oneida, as "built like a hydrant and wearing a little short cap"', bounded out of bed and tried to awaken her husband.

"Abe", she shouted, "get up." However Moon was completely anesthetized and slept blissfully on.

Chloe Ann started after Rivers, shouting at the top of her voice. The burglars, seeing it was useless to try to quiet her, fled. They walked out the kitchen door with Chloe Ann at their heels, scolding.

When she returned to the sitting room she tripped over her husband's pants on the floor. "Abe, where are you?" she cried, "Abe, what are you doing."

Her husband slumbered blissfully on in his bed. By this time the rest of the household was awakened. It was too late. The two thieves had gone. The sack of money Moon had tossed under the table was found safe.

As Rivers and Jacques were driving toward Wampsville, they found a wagon and horse following them. The wagon was loaded with roistering youth. The two thieves thought they were being pursued. They whipped up their horse. When they reached Wampsville, they abandoned the horse and carriage, and ran cross lots and caught the New York Central Railroad train to Syracuse.

Rivers and Jacques were unaware that their "pursuers" were neighborhood youths returning home from a dance.

The next morning William Crumb of Wampsville found the abandoned horse and wagon. He unhitched the horse and put it in his barn. A neighbor, who examined the carriage, found some of the Moon's silver was lying on the bottom. Upon learning of the robbery, suspicion fell on Crumb and he was arrested. He posted bail. As Crumb had a good reputation, he was soon cleared of the crime and released.

Rivers and Jacques turned their loot over to the Earl brothers when they reached Syracuse. James Bryan, who believed the gang planned to do him out of his share, went to the police.

Members of the gang were arrested. A search of their Franklin Street home disclosed buffalo robes, blankets, whips, men and women's apparel and even a quantity of butter. Much of it was identified as stolen from other homes.

The gang was brought to trial in Onondaga County Court in February, 1881 and the members were found guilty. Leon Earl, the leader, was sentenced to sixty-five years in Auburn Prison by Judge Reigel. Charles Earl received twenty five years and his wife, Emma, fifteen years. Jacques and Rivers also received long sentences. Bryan who turned in the gang, received a five-year sentence.

Leon Earl served twenty five years of his sentence before he was pardoned by Governor Odell on April 15, 1902.

After Rivers served his sentence, he often returned to the Cowaselone Valley to visit old friends. However, he stayed clear of the Moon home.

DEATH ALONG THE CANAL

On that day, August 28, 1837, when Robert Barber left his home in Coleraine, Massachusetts to travel to Onondaga Valley in Upstate New York to marry Miss Betsey Taggert, there was nothing to indicate his journey would terminate in Madison County.

Miss Taggert was about forty six years of age. A native of Coleraine, she had moved to Onondaga Valley in 1824. Barber, who was in his early fifty's and a widower, had known his fiancee for several years. He had proposed by mail, and being accepted, had left his children and other relatives to make the journey.

After traveling by stage, Barber reached Utica, the following day. It was here he met Lewis Wilbur, who was about twenty one years of age. Wilbur claimed Saratoga as his home. Although accounts claim Wilbur was "a low and vicious character and in the habit of thieving from childhood", he must have been well-dressed and acted as a gentleman to become acquainted with Barber.

Wilbur purchased a long-bladed knife, known as a "dirk" in a Utica store. He carefully wrapped the knife in paper and hid it in the shirt pocket of his coat. He already carried a pistol concealed on his person.

Wilbur purchased Barber he should book passage on a packet boat on the Erie Canal instead of continuing on the turnpike to Onondaga Valley. The canal was slower than the stage, Wilbur said, but it would mean a smoother ride than over the bumpy road. Barber agree. He and Wilbur purchased passage on a line boat going west that night, August 29. The boat was captained by Edwin H. Munger.

The boat reached Rome later that evening. The following morning, Captain Munger tied up at Burr's Tavern in Sullivan, about three miles east of Chittenango Landing.

Barber and Wilbur went ashore together and had a drink in the tavern. The older man was wearing his dress clothing as he expected to greet Miss Taggert sometime in the afternoon. He had on snuff-colored pantoloons, a brown vest, a pleated stock around his neck, a straight-bodied coat, a little darker

111

than his pantaloons. He had on a new pair of calfskin boots and a hat.

Wilbur suggested a walk for exercise, and Barber agreed. They took the towpath until they reached Lee's Bridge, west of the tavern. After crossing the bridge they started walking slowly along the highway. They passed a fork in the road that led off south to Canaseraga on the Genesee Turnpike, and continued on until the last farm buildings and open fields were passed and they came to a woods. Wilbur suggested they walk through the woods and Barber agreed.

The men climbed over the split rail fence and walked along a woods road. When they were about sixty rods off the main highway, Wilbur pulled out his pistol and pointed it at Barber. At the same time he reached down and pulled the dirk from his coat tail pocket.

Although the pistol was empty, Wilbur kept it on the older man, and excitedly demanded all the money he was carrying. Barber took out his pocketbook from inside his coat and a purse of coins from his pocket.

"I did not think that of you," Barber said nervously. "I thought you were my friend."

"Throw them on the ground," the youth instructed. Barber complied. "Lay down," Wilbur commanded, "and hide your face and don't look up for half an hour."

The frightened man obeyed, and Wilbur picked up the pocketbook and purse. Wilbur confessed later that as he stood looking down on the man lying face down in the dirt before him with his right arm under his eyes, a thought warned him of the danger of detection if he allowed Barber to live.

"If the old gentleman had made the least resistance or noise, I would have fled and left him untouched," he said.

Barber remained silent. Wilbur suddenly leaned over and pulled up the older man's coat and plunged his dirk into the helpless body. Wilbur plunged the knife several more times into Barber's back. When the older man made no outcry, Wilbur picked up a large stone nearby and smashed Barber's skull.

After making certain there was no blood on his hands or clothing, Wilbur returned to the boat and went on to Buffalo.

Barber was not missed by Captain Munger until his trunk went unclaimed when the boat tied up at Buffalo. The captain returned his boat to Albany and reported the missing man.

Suspicion that Barber was murdered rested on Wilbur, who had been his companion.

Search parties scoured both sides of the canal from Lee's Bridge to Chittenango Landing the following October, but the body of the missing man was not found.

Winter came and was almost over, when in March, 1838, the partly decomposed body of Barber was discovered by Harley Judd and several men from Chittenango Landing.

A warrant for the arrest of Wilbur was issued. Posters containing his description were circulated. The story of the murder was carried by newspapers throughout the country.

Wilbur was arrested in the Town of Medina, Ohio in April, where he was living under the name of Lewis Lee. He was brought back to Madison County and lodged in the county jail at Morrisville.

He was indicted at the court of General Sessions of the Peace on "the third Monday of June, 1838, before Edward Rogers, Barak Bickwitte, Joseph Clark, Epenitus Holmes and Horatio G. Warner, Judges of the county courts, for the murder of Robert Barber, on August 30, 1837."

District Attorney Justin Dwinell prosecuted, assisted by Attorneys B. D. Noxon and Timothy Jenkins. J. A. Spencer and A. L. Foster were Wilbur' attorneys.

The jury returned its verdict on May 23, and Judge Monell pronounced the death sentence, Wilbur should be hung by the neck until dead. The date for the execution was set for October 3, 1839.

On September 24, only nine days before the death date Attorneys Spencer and Foster brought action against the county for a retrial. They based their action on three affidavits that the jurors had been served "spirituous liquors" while staying at the house of Henry Dewey during the trial. William L. Thompson, barkeeper in the Dewey House, testified taking up a bottle of rum and a bottle of brandy, with tumblers, sugar and water. Each bottle contained about a pint, he said.

Daison Harkell of the Town of Fenner and Nathaniel C. Gregg of the Town of Stockbridge, both members of the jury, also swore to affidavits. After the jury had returned its verdict, Joseph Spencer, paid Thompson ten shillings for the two bottles.

The court reaffirmed the verdict found by the jurors.

The day of the hanging was a county holiday. Thousands of persons came from the surrounding townships and the roads were clogged with horses and teams. Many of the people had brought lunches and waited patiently for the militia to escort the prisoner from the jail to the scaffold.

Wilbur's feelings frequently overcame his ability to talk. He groaned, wept and writhed trying to escape the noose as it was placed over his head. At last the trap was sprung and he was launched into eternity.

A FIVE MINUTE VISIT

Abraham Lincoln appeared briefly to the huge crowd that had gathered in Little Falls, when his train arrived in February 18, 1861. Grandpa Elderbert Walter heard him speak.

Grandpa was eight years old at the time, but he always managed to recall Lincoln's appearance and the words he spoke. Grandpa had been driven to Little Falls by his parents, Mr. and Mrs. William Walter of Newville. Some of his brothers and sisters were also along.

Lincoln was enroute from his home in Springfield, Illinois, to Washington, D. C. to be sworn into the presidency. His train had made stops in Syracuse, Rome and Utica before coming to Little Falls. All along the way the president-elect and his family were greeted by admiring crowds. He spoke briefly in the cities where the train stopped and shook hands with the officials who were allowed aboard the train to meet him.

Grandpa Walter recalled how tall and ungainly the bearded new president looked, but when he spoke a hush fell over the crowd.

Lincoln was well aware he was entering the most critical and difficult phase of his life. Great responsibilities loomed ahead. Nevertheless he had a smile and a joke for the thousands who had turned out to greet him.

It was ten minutes past noon on February 10, when his train arrived at the New York Central Railroad Station in Little Falls. Cannons boomed and a newly formed brass band played "Hail Columbia" but the sound was almost drowned out by the cheering crowds. Several hundred women, who were in the forefront near the train began waving hankerchiefs in unison.

S. M. Richmond, the village president, extended the official greetings to the president-elect.

Lincoln spoke briefly: "Ladies and gentlemen, I appear before you merely for the purpose of greeting you and saying a few words and bidding you farewell. I can only say as I have often said before that I have no speech to make and no time to make one, if I had. Neither have I the strength to repeat a speech at all the places at which I stop, even though the circumstances were favorable.

"I am thankful for this opportunity of seeing you and allowing you to see me," he said, "and in this, so far as regards to the ladies I think I have the best of the bargain. I don't make that acknowledgement, however, to the gentlemen. And now, I believe I really have made my speech and am ready to bid you farewell when the train moves on."

At the end of his remarks, the applause thundered over the valley.

Mr. Lincoln seemed well-pleased with the turnout. Within a short time he was to need the backing of every citizen.

A reporter from the Albany Journal who was traveling with the presidential party, wrote: "At Little Falls took place what was pronounced the prettiest brief reception that President Lincoln has received since he left Springfield and that pleasantly attested that the go-ahead citizens of Little Falls were ready and proud to do all they could in five minutes to attest their loyalty to the president-elect. The love of the great man and the undying zeal in behalf of the institutions he has called by the voice of the people to preserve and defend."

The Little Falls Journal and Courier said, "Those who saw the smile about his countenance wondered how the face could be called homely. And all who heard his manly voice knew intuitively that it was the voice of an honest man."

The train began slowly to leave the station as the crowds cheered and the brass band played. Lincoln remained on the rear platform waving as the train gathered speed, carrying him to his destiny.

THE FORGOTTEN BRAKEMAN

The neighbors thought old John Elphick was somewhat peculiar, but children loved to hear his stories about when he was the first brakeman on the first steam train in New York State.

Elphick, his wife and two children moved to Poolville, in Madison County in 1849 when his days of railroading were ended.

Older residents remembered that the old man worked at several jobs, including janitor of the Methodist Episcopal Church.

He kept some cows and had a few acres of land that he worked outside the hamlet. His daughter, Miss Lucy J. Elphick, tended the cows. She set their milk in pans and skimmed off the cream and made butter in a dash churn and sold it to neighbors.

T. D. Stebbins, recalling his childhood said, "Mr. Elphick was very strict about doing a good job."

"If us kids did a little too much walking around and too much loud talking he would order us outdoors saying, "This is a church, not a playground.' For that reason we thought he was an old crank," Mr. Stebbins said.

"He would tell us kids of his railroad experiences. We listened very earnestly to every word," he continued. "He used to tell us about taking out the first train. Probably the way he expressed his work lead me to think he was an engineer."

For many years Mr. Elphick worked for Henry Berry in his cannery. He was a very hard working man. Mr. Berry was well off and did not work much, but sat in his office.

"One day, Mr. Berry said to Elphick, 'I would give anything if I could work as you do.' "

His employee looked at him without smiling. "It depends a lot on whether you have to or not," he answered.

Mr. Elphick was born in Battle, England, September 21, 1812, one of nine children. On April 9, 1830, at the age of seventeen, he embarked on the brig William, owned by a Captain Williams and his sister, at Rye, England. Elphick arrived in New York City on June 19 of that year.

The slim youth found employment as a laborer with the New Mohawk and Hudson Railroad Co.

The company was chartered in 1826 to build the rail line, but actual construction did not start until 1830. The contract to make the roadbed and lay the rails was held by John Littlejohn, Colonel Barker and James Myers. John B. Jervis was superintendent of construction. The capital to build the road the sixteen miles between Albany and Schenectady was put up by moneyed men from New York City.

The rails were length of iron on heavy wooden pieces that were strapped to heavy blocks of granite.

Elphick was a brakeman on the horse-drawn construction train that hauled materials for the line. He worked 12 hours a day and received 37½ cents a day and his board for salary. George Shaw, the overseer of the construction crew, was the envy of the other laborers as he received 50 cents a day. These were considered "good living wages" as board and lodging could be had for a dollar a week.

Three miles of the road, a part of each terminal, were so steep that it was thought advisable to use horse power. Stationary engines were placed at the top of the hills and the train was hauled up and down by means of a rope.

The DeWitt Clinton, the engine built for the railroad at the West Point Foundry, was about 12 feet in length, with large wheels, a central dome, and a large smokestack. The engineer stood on a platform at the rear. A small flat car was attached to the engine. This carried a stack of cut cordwood to fire the boiler, and two hogsheads of water connected to the engine by a leather hose.

On Monday, August 9, 1831, according to the Albany Argus, "the 'DeWitt Clinton' attached to a train of cars, passed over the road from plane to plane, to the delight of a large crowd assembled to witness the performance. the engine performed the entire route in less than one hour, including stoppages, and on a part of the road its speed was at the rate of thirty miles an hour."

The train was made up of three converted stage coaches as passenger cars and six flat cars, each connected to the other with pieces of chain.

Before the train started, William H. Brown, an itinerant silhouette artist, was perched on a high spot overlooking the crowd. Using his flat-topped beaver hat as a desk top, he carefully sketched the train and its passengers on a piece of paper.

The silhouette that Brown made of the first steam train ever to travel in New York State was remarkable for its accuracy. However, the caption under its reproduction on posters and in newspapers has confused historians. It contained a number of inaccuracies. The DeWitt Clinton was called the John Bull, an imported British engine. David Matthew, a former Schenectady liveryman, who was the engineer, was identified as John Hampson of England. The passengers, who included Thurlow Weed, the renowned Albany newspaper editor; ex-Governor Joseph C. Yates, and Jacob Hayes, high constable of New York City, were all drawn accurately. However John Elphick, the brakeman, is not shown.

Elphick married the former Sarah J. Curtis in October, 1833. He remained with the railroad until he moved to Poolville with his family. Besides his daughter, Lucy, he had a son, Fayette Elphick, who became a doctor and also served as postmaster of Stockbridge.

Mr. Elphick worked hard the rest of his life. He died in May, 1909 at the age of 97.

THE STONE BARN

The old Stone Barn has taken on new life.

Like the ruins of a medieval castle, the huge stone barn rises from the pastureland at the end of Stone Barn Road, near the hamlet of Jewell. For years the ruins have been a favorite subject for artists as well as upstate newspaper feature writers.

The ruins of the cobblestone home-barn building and adjacent land were purchased in 1970 by Dr. Robert W. Hugel, who is well-known in Oneida County mental health circles.

Dr. Hugel and Miss E. Alison Joeckel of Yorkshire, England, were married in the barn in September, 1970 by Town of Vienna Justice Arthur Sable. Among the guests at the wedding were Mr. and Mrs. Andrew H. Brockway of Cleveland, who were married in the building in September, 1925. Mrs. Brockway's parents occupied the estate at that time.

Dr. and Mrs. Hugel have started reconstruction of the house part of the barn.

For many years Utica and Syracuse newspapermen claimed the barn was the basis for Walter Edmonds excellent novel. "The Big Barn" or as it was renamed in the paperback edition, "The Magnificent Wilders."

Edmonds evidently used a big barn built on the Lyman R. Lyons farm at Lyons Falls in 1859 or 1860 as the basis for his theme. The timbers were hand hewn from hemlock trees on the farm and the limestone for the foundation was hauled on sleighs across the ice-covered river during the winter from the quarry. More than 300 men helped with the barn raisin'. The barn had about sixteen "vents" or sections of frame work.

"High Falls" as mentioned by Edmonds in his book, was the early name of Lyons Falls.

The character of Lyman R. Lyons is similar to that of Ralph Wilder while the character of "Bascom" of the story is said to be similar to that of Caleb Lyon, a younger brother of Lyman.

The "Stone Barn" as it was called by its owner, Charles W. Knight of Rome, a prominent civil engineer, was started in 1899. It was completed in 1906 at a cost of $140,000.

The barn was 120 feet long and 42 feet in width and covered 24,000 square feet. More than 500 cords of cobblestones, fine hardwoods and wrought iron were used.

The main part of the building was the barn. It housed fifty cows. In front of each stall was a manger, built of stone and cement, and an individual drinking fountain. The fountains were automatically supplied with fresh water drawn by windmills from a nearby spring-fed brook and forced into a reservoir at the top of the barn.

Under the smooth cement floor a huge ventilating tube with registers, was constructed to carry off the barn odors to the chimneys at the eastern end of the structure.

The western end of the building contained the living quarters. A modern creamery was built over a root cellar. A stone ice house and smoke house and several wooden-frame tenant houses were also constructed on the property.

Laborers who worked on the barn received a dollar for an eleven-hour work day. Henry Griesmeyer, the stone mason boss, received $1.50. Teamsters received $3 a day.

Knight housed a purebred herd of dairy cattle in the barn and shipped certified milk by way of the New York, Ontario and Western Railway to New York City. High quality butter was also sent.

Knight operated his dairy farm for eleven years at a loss of considerable money. He finally abandoned the project.

The barn stood empty for a number of years with the exception of a short period in which a family occupied the living quarters in the west end of the building.

It finally came into the possession of Eugene Westcott of Cleveland who used it to house race horses. The great racer Delwina is reported to have been born there. Her son, Prince Delwina ran in many races at Vernon Downs.

During the early 1940's the barn and 513 acres of land were sold to Joseph Buda of Canastota.

The barn was swept by a mysterious fire on March 23, 1946. The entire interior was destroyed. The heat was so intense firemen could not stand within 500 feet of the structure.

Only the castle-like ruins were left to become a subject for painters and photographers. An attempt was made to commercialize the ruins as an amusement park in May, 1957, under the name of "Stone Barn Enterprises", at an estimated cost of $25,000. Although the park was opened, it did not last too many years.

Today, under the new owners, the stone barn has been given a new lease on life.

BURNED AT THE STAKE

Older residents of the Mohawk Valley have told me that witches do not ride broomsticks any more. They also claim that women and not men are "consorts of the devil," but there is no way of accurately telling them from ordinary mortals. Halloween, Friday the 13th, and midnight, the witching hour, so long associated with witchcraft, have no real significance. Witches have no particular hours or days in which to indulge in their nefarious pranks.

A Negro woman, accused and condemned as a witch, was burned at the stake in 1774 in the jail yard in Johnstown, Montgomery County.

The slave was owned by Christian Nellis of Johnstown. She burned her master's buildings. When she was captured, all she could say was, "The devil come to me in the night and made me do it."

She was tried as a witch in Johnstown and was ordered to be burned at the stake. After the sentence was carried out, Nellis sued for property damage and recovered the cost of the slave.

THE LONELY GRAVE

On Mount Pisgah, one of the hills in the northeastern part of the Town of Nelson, a small, upright slab of stone marks the lonely grave of an early road-builder.

The grave of Randall Grover overlooks the valley below. It is located near the deeply-rutted and overgrown, grass-covered remains of the old state road. In the spring and summer, the tiger lilies and lilacs still bloom near the empty cellar ruins of the "village" of Argus.

Grover, who was a young man, is only a name. Nothing is known of his family nor where he lived. He was employed, along with Ezra Booth, later a pioneer settler, and several other men, to cut a road from Pratt's Settlement (Pratts Hollow) southeast across the hills to meet the Old State Road, or Lincklaen Road, as it was also known, at Argus. This was probably about 1800. No records of the road exist today.

The axmen were cutting a large swath through the forest Booth recalled later. Three massive trees that were cut fell into each other and were held upright by a smaller tree.

The trees had to be dropped. Grover and Booth walked up to them. Grover lifted his ax and swung one blow at the uncut tree. The impact sent the three trees crashing downward. Booth leaped aside as the branches scraped his clothing. Grover, somewhat bewildered, jumped two or three steps toward safety when one of the huge trees crashed down on him.

"Grover is a dead man!" Booth cried.

The other axmen rushed to the tree and found Grover crushed beneath it.

The men buried him nearby the road.

Booth became an early settler of Nelson and died there June 3, 1866.

THE BENNET MURDER

John (Jack) Maxwell came home from prison in 1871 and found his wife, Mary, in bed with her lover and shot him.

Maxwell worked on the Erie Canal as a boatman and like William "Bill" Alvord, stole horses and other produce for the Loomis Gang. Nothing is known of his early life. He was arrested for stealing horses about 1865, near Higginsville in Oneida County. Maxwell was convicted of the charge and sent to State Prison.

While serving the term, his wife, the former Mary Donahue of New London, took up with William Bennet. Mrs. Maxwell and Bennet lived together as man and wife in Durhamville for one canal season, then moved to Oneida and later to South Bay. Mrs. Maxwell bore Bennet two children, a boy and girl. The boy, about three years old, died in March 1971. Shortly before the boy's death, the couple resided in Rochester for the summer.

Mrs. Maxwell left Rochester and went to visit her mother in Fayetteville.

Maxwell was released from prison in 1870 and expressed a desire to live with his wife again. Mrs. Mary Maxwell refused to accept him as her husband. Her two children called Bennet "father" and she looked upon her lover as her husband.

After the death of her son, Mrs. Maxwell returned to the Durhamville area to visit her brother-in-law and sister, Mr. and Mrs. Hugh Kenyon, who resided across the canal from Durhamville, in the Town of Lenox in Madison County. She told her sister she and her lover were preparing to go west.

Bennet, who was employed in a brickyard in Rochester, came to Oneida on Thursday night, September 28, 1871. He walked from Oneida to the Kenyon home, arriving sometime between 10 and 12 o'clock that night.

Early Friday morning Maxwell came to the Kenyon home. He found his wife and Bennet together in bed and their two-year old daughter in the same room. Maxwell pulled a revolver he was carrying and fired four shots at Bennet. Two of them hit their mark. Before a physician could be called, Bennet was dead.

Maxwell fled the scene going to Durhamville. Officers were quickly on his trail. Later that Friday night he was arrested in a barn near Camden.

Deputy Sheriff Simon S. Hart of Madison County, said "(I) went to arrest Maxwell with Squire Palmer."

"During the day of the murder the prisoner slept in a barn near the Loomis property," Hart recalled. "When the prisoner was arrested (he) did not appear unusually excited. I took the pistol from him. It was loaded."

Dr. Henry C. Carpenter, of Oneida, Madison County coroner, held an inquest on Bennet Saturday. Maxwell was charged with willful murder and he was committed to the County Jail in Morrisville.

Early in October, 1871, Maxwell was indicted by the Grand Jury for murder. He pleaded not guilty to the charge upon arraignment. He was represented by attorneys I. N. Messinger of Oneida and J. C. Kennedy of Morrisville.

The murder trial began on May 1, 1872, with Justice Douglas Boardman of the Supreme Court presiding and Nathan Brown and Asher McRay, justices of Sessions.

The jury was composed of Edwin Crandall, Atwell Walkee, Major A. Smith, John Cook, Frank Isbell, Delos B. Collester, Alanson C. Wilcox, Warren Williams, Philo Parker, William Farnham and William Stanbro.

District Attorney Gerrit A. Forbes presented as the Peoples Witnesses, Edwin Donahue, Ann Kenyon, Hugh Kenyon, Frank Bortle, Attorney B. Franklin Chapman, James Stevens, Jefferson Adle, Ezra Cline, Nathan Mills, Charles Ackerman, William W. Warner, Samuel Frank, Simon S. Harp, Lucius C. Palmer, Martin L. Case, Lawrence Barnard, Horace J. Noble, Frank Donahue, Daniel Pine, Jacob H. Parsons, Nancy Cunningham, Adellon B. Brown, Albert C. Purdy and Dr. Henry C. Carpenter.

Barnard testified that he resided at Buffalo and was a boatman. "Maxwell worked for me until the 27th of September when I settled with him."

The testimony given also brought out that Maxwell was known as Robert Cunningham while he was in prison. He had been sentenced to four years and six months for horse stealing and served the sentence.

Witnesses presented by the defense were: Asa LaClear, Silas LaClear, John Sheets, John F. Hager Jr., Oliver Sheets

Frances LaBarnard, William H. Stenson, Frank Hosley, Harmon Eddy, John B. Gray and Byron Tubbs. Maxwell also took the stand in his defense.

The court convened at the ringing of the bell at 12 o'clock noon, on May 3, 1872 to report they had found the prisoner "Guilty of murder in the first degree."

Justice Boardman sentenced Maxwell "to be hung between the hours of nine in the morning and three in the afternoon of June 21, 1872 in some private field or enclosure of said jail until he is dead."

Despite Maxwell's criminal background, his wife's perfidy gained him much sympathy.

Eleven days before he was to be hanged his sentence was commuted to imprisonment for life. The Utica Morning Herald on May 16, 1879, add this footnote, "He has since died."

WOMAN AERONAUT

The weather was excellent for a balloon ascension that summer day in 1876 in Hamilton. At the foot of the park, Dr. William Mann was busily instructing his crew who were inflating his balloon, the "Chenango."

About four o'clock one of the crew members announced to the crowd Dr. Mann would not make the ascent. Instead, one of his pupils, Miss Mindy Williams of Sherburne, would make her first flight.

Miss Williams, a slender, attractive woman of 29 came forth. She carried a large American flag in her hands. She was helped to enter the wicker basket.

Arminda Robenia Williams prided herself on being an independent thinker. She was employed as a telegraph operator in Sherburne. She became interested in balloon ascentions and pursuaded Dr. Mann to accept her as a pupil.

She smiled and waved the flag as the balloon began its ascent. It took a southeasterly direction rising about a mile in height and drifting about two miles. The balloon rose suddenly as if some of the ballast had been dropped shooting upward out of sight in the clouds.

The balloon continued to drift eastward and suddenly reappeared from a rift in the clouds. She landed safely near Dowell's Corners after a ride of about twenty five minutes about three miles from Poolville. Miss Williams was picked up by a man with a horse and carriage and driven to that hamlet. From there she boarded a Delaware, Lackawanna and Western train that took her home to Sherburne.

Miss Williams made several other flights, some from the Sherburne Fairgrounds. At one time the basket landed in a farm tree near Poolville but she escaped uninjured.

At the Sherburne Fair held in August, 1872 the wind was too strong for a balloon ascension. Dr. Mann began filling his "Chenango", but unknowingly, it was blown against some sharp objects causing rents in the fabric.

Miss Williams evidently did not plan on making an ascent. She had an excellent hair wreath on exhibition in the women's section.

THE WHITE MEN'S FRIENDS

A silk and horsehair shawl and a boulder bearing a plaque are all that is left today to recall a brave Oneida Indian woman and a chief who aided the colonists in their fight for freedom during the Revolution.

The shawl belonged to Polly Cooper. The boulder indicates about where the home of Chief Skenandoah stood near the Great Western Turnpike in Oneida Castle.

Little is known of Polly Cooper. Chief William Rockwell, her great, great grandson, (now deceased) said she was born at Oneida Castle.

When Washington's rag-tag army was slowly starving to death at Valley Forge, several Oneida Indians carried 600 bags of corn to them. Polly Cooper went along to show how the corn should be prepared. She is also said to have cooked for Washington.

At the close of the Revolution, the Oneidas were offered pay for their contribution, but it was refused.

Polly Cooper said, "I was born free. I refuse to take pay for it, as I too, fought for freedom."

Her descendants have two versions on how she obtained the shawl. One account is that she saw the black diaphanous shawl and a bonnet in a store window in Philadelphia and mentioned to the soldiers how much she would like to have them.

In the spring of 1778 after she returned to her home at the Castle, two soldiers from Washington's army "rode up and presented her with the shawl and bonnet."

The other story is that some members of Congress, wishing to honor Polly for her contribution, asked Mrs. Benjamin Franklin to select a suitable gift. The shawl and bonnet were chosen.

The bonnet disappeared many years ago. The shawl is presently owned by Mrs. Louella Derrick, a descendant, who resides on the Onondaga Reservation. Mrs. Derrick keeps the shawl in a Syracuse bank vault.

Polly Cooper is believed to have married a brother of Chief Skenandoah. Chief Rockwell said she spent the remainder of her life among her people. Her death date and burial place are unknown.

Chief Rockwell said, "She was a handsome woman."

A seven-ton granite boulder at High Bridge, between Oneida Castle and Sherrill, stands near the last home of Chief Skenandoah. It was dedicated by Skenandoah Chapter of the American Revolution in 1912.

The Chief died March 11, 1816, aged about 110 years and is buried beside his friend, the Rev. Samuel Kirkland, the noted missionary, in the Hamilton College Cemetery, near Clinton.

Among the last words credited to the Chief, was this paragraph, which has been quoted many times:

"I am an aged hemlock; the winds of a hundred winters have whistled through my branches; I am dead at the top. The generation to which I belonged have run away and left me; why I live the Great Spirit only knows; pray to my Jesus that I may have patience to wait for my appointed time to die."

The date of the chief's birth, his parents and early life are veiled with the mists of time. He was born about 1700 and is believed to have belonged to some other tribe, possibly the Conestogas and was adopted by the Oneidas at an early age.

During the Revolution Chief Skenandoah, like the majority of the Oneida Nation, sided with the colonists. The remainder of the great Iroquois Confederacy sided with Great Britian and were led by Chief Joseph Brant of the Mohawks.

Chief Skenandoah and another Oneidan, Thomas Spencer, who also resided at the Oneida Castle, were with General Herkimer at the battle of Oriskany. Spencer lost his life fighting in the ambush.

In appearance Skenandoah was more than six feet in height and well proportioned. He had nine lines of tattooing running across his shoulders and chest. Skenandoah was noted for his strength and endurance. He was ruling chief among the Oneidas.

In 1755 he was present during the treaty making in Albany. Three years later when the Chevalier de Belstrie headed a party of 300 French and Indians from Oswegatchie to attack Herkimer and the German Flatts, Skenandoah notified the residents. The settlers who were lulled by a false sense of security failed to heed his warning and were slaughtered.

Skenandoah aided Sir William Johnson in dictating the measures and wise, cautious policy which brought the Indian agent, his appointment of Royal Superintendent of Indian Affairs.

During his youth Skenandoah was wild and intemperate. When attending the treaty making in Albany in 1755, Skenandoah became gloriously drunk. When he awakened, he found he had been stripped of his clothing and his head sheared. Seeing himself in a looking glass, he was shocked by his appearance. He vowed never again to taste the debasing firewater of the white man. It was a vow he religiously kept.

During his declining years, he gave his people this advice, "Drink no strong water. It makes mice for white men, who are cats. Many a meal have they eaten of you!"

Dominie Samuel Kirkland was responsible for Skenandoah's embracing Christianity. Their friendship lasted a lifetime. After the Revolution, Hugh White, the pioneer settler of Whitestown, consulted with the Chief about settling on the frontier.

Skenandoah resided at this time in a small house in the butternut grove at Oneida Castle. He kept a small store.

The Rev. Mather Cooley of Granville, Massachusetts, spent a day among the Oneidas. He wrote afterwards, "They live in huts poorly constructed and mostly covered by bark. They raise a little corn, but are not fond of husbandry. They are 700 in number and receive about seven dollars annuity from the state for their lands. This keeps them drunk for a number of days.

"I visited Skenandoah, an old chief. His house is red. Within it is well furnished with skins and blankets and smells strong of the game and the woods. I had no interpreter and could not converse with them."

Skenandoah had many distinguished visitors to his home, including Governor Clinton.

After the Rev. Kirkland removed to Clinton, Skenandoah expressed a desire to be buried at the side of his friend.

During his many visits to Clinton the old Chief was treated with great kindness by the Kirkland family.

Chief Skenandoah's last sickness came upon him when he was at his home at Oneida Castle. Prayers were offered at his bedside by his great granddaughter. He died peacefully.

A large funeral cortege accompanied the Chief's body to Clinton. He was buried beside his white friend.

MIRACLE WOMAN

Mrs. Deiadamia Button Chase of Brookfield began working miracles with her medicines concocted from roots, herbs and spices in the 1820's and 1830's at a time when male physicians were purging, blistering and bleeding.

Mrs. Chase was also clairvoyant and studied Phrenology. Born in Brookfield in 1802, she was the daughter of John and Polly Button. Mrs. Chase learned the medicinal value of roots and herbs from her grandmother, Mrs. Anna Button, who was a midwife. In 1814 when a fever epidemic swept the countryside, John Button was strickened. The girl dosed him with "spice bush" or "fever bush tea", as it is also known, and saved his life.

When Deiadamia was fourteen, her father was seriously injured when a tree fell on him while he and some of his neighbors were clearing a woodlot. Button never recovered. He developed inflammation of the brain. Deiadamia and a cousin were sitting up with him one night when the house suddenly shook as if struck with a cannon ball. The girls could hear the mysterious "ball" as it seemed to drop from the garret to the cellar. The girls searched the house and even checked out of doors, but found nothing.

Deiadamia was worried if the noise had disturbed her father. "My daughter," he said "don't be frightened. It is a warning of my death."

Button died a short time afterwards. Deiadamia and her brother, John Avery Button, were left destitute and went to live with relatives. The girl went to reside with her mother's sister. The aunt and uncle were extremely penurious. When Deiadamia became ill, her aunt refused to call the doctor, saying her uncle would have to pay the bill.

Her grandmother hearing of the cruel treatment, took the girl to live with her.

Deiadamia had several offers of marriage, but turned them all down. When she was twenty she met a handsome young man, who seemed to have many of her father's qualities. His name was Orrin Chase and he resided in the Town of Winfield, Herkimer County. They were married April 23, 1822 at the home of Mrs. Brown, a widowed aunt of the bride.

After their marriage, Chase purchased a farm in the wilderness near Georgetown. The young bride became ill with inflamation of the brain. A local physician was called and he bled and blistered her. Although she recovered, she carried the scars of the physician's ignorance the remainder of her life.

Mrs. Chase gave birth to her first child in March, 1826. She was to have seven more children. Her daughter, Luna, who was born in February, 1835, was to grow up and became Mrs. Hammond, a historian and writer.

The canker rash raged in the neighborhood in 1834 and almost every case proved fatal. Chase was away on business when two of the children became ill with the disease. She hoped her eight-year old son would not catch it, but he came home from school complaining of a sore throat.

Mrs. Chase examined the children's throats and saw each was covered by a rash. She knelt in prayer, while unconsciously rubbing her own throat. When she opened her eyes she saw the leaves of a burdock growing near the door. On impulse, she picked some of the leaves and laid them on the stove until they withered. She steamed them with vinegar and bound the wet leaves around her childrens' throats.

The next morning every sign of the rash was gone from her son's throat. The eldest daughter also recovered, but the youngest nearly died. The canker ate holes in her neck until her bones and cords were laid bare. Chase returned home and immediately sought a physician. The doctor gave the couple no hope. When he left, Mrs. Chase knelt in prayer. Again, moved by impulse, she removed the bandages from her daughter's neck and laid her hands soothingly over the sores. The girl seemed to breathe easier and soon dropped off into a restful slumber.

The doctor was surprised to see the change in his patient when he returned the next day. He asked Mrs. Chase if she had given the child the medicine he had left. She replied she had not.

"Well let it be what it is you have given her," he said. "The child is decidedly better. I have reason to believe she will recover."

The cankerous sores were healed within three days. In a week the child was able to be playing about the house.

The Chase's six-week old child was attacked with a severe cough in 1835. The infant's spasms became so severe, death seemed imminent. The mother received another impulse. She prepared some Lungwort and started giving it in small doses to the baby. Within a few days the infant was completely cured. Mrs. Chase had never known or heard of a cure for the disease previously.

While residents of Georgetown, Chase embraced religion and was baptised into the Free Baptist Church. At the communion, Rev. Hall, the pastor, invited all to commune with them who were on "Gospel grounds". "Those who deny the Trinity, or believe in Universal Salavation, we do not consider as being on Gospel grounds, and we exclude them," he said.

Mrs. Chase did not take communion. She was a member of the Unitarian Church. She asked herself, "why is it that a disciple of Christ — a brother christian — should forbid me the fellowship of communion, and thereby insinuate that I am no christian?"

Several members of the Free Baptist Church and Rev. Hall asked her to forsake her religion and join with them.

In the neighborhood there resided a woman who was considered insane, for she had a gift of prophecy. The woman seemed to be able to read a person's thoughts as soon as she looked upon them. Upon seeing Rev. Hall, the woman said to Mrs. Chase, "There is Elder Hall, he will be as black as the wall —."

Nothing was ever known about the pastor's character and he maintained an excellent reputation in the community. The woman's words came back to Mrs. Chase several years later when Rev. Hall eloped with a married woman and he was dropped from the list of ministers.

When Luna Chase was three years of age she accidentally fell into a kettle of boiling water. Having on heavy woolen clothing, the child was scalded very deeply before her clothes could be removed. The family did not seek a physician. The first night Mr. and Mrs. Chase sat up with the child and kept applying poultices made of grated potatoes. The next morning Mrs. Chase gave the child oil to keep her bowels regular.

Although she cleansed the burns, inflammation set in. Mrs. Chase made a poultice of black or striped maple bark steeped in milk and water, after which she threw in a handful of beech leaves, allowing them to soak until they were soft. Then she added tallow to the mixture to prevent it from sticking to the sores. She spread this on her child's body, allowing the beech leaves to lay next to the sores.

The preparation extracted all the soreness and large sloughs of putrid flesh came off with each dressing until the edges of the sores were clean and healing.

Mr. Chase was afraid the girl's limbs would become stiffened. To alleviate this, she manipulated the limbs daily, applying ointment on the cords. In six weeks, Luna was able to stand and use her limbs.

In the early 1840's Mr. and Mrs. Chase moved from Georgetown to Nelson. Their three oldest children had married. A son was left on the farm. A "friend" of Chase's who held the $1,000 mortgage on the farm sold the place. The Chase family had almost reached the bottom of the ladder.

The couple were religious, but never settled down to become good members of any one denomination. Mrs. Chase's interest in Phrenology became known, a member of the Free Will Baptist Church called her an "infidel."

Elder Judd worried about Mrs. Chase and visited her. She explained about the science and offered to examine his head. The preacher accepted. When she completed her study, Elder Judd told her to continue with her work.

The minister's endorsement opened the doors for her to many homes. Through her studies she was able to diagnose several illnesses and effect cures. Mrs. Chise became known as a clairvoyant.

In 1850 she was mesmerized several times during the winter by A. P. Cook. While in her trances she clearly showed she possessed powers of a great degree.

As an example, in 1849, before the neighbors became aware of her powers, one of Mrs. Chase's lady boarders asked her to examine her head. Mrs. Chase began her examination and then stopped.

"What! a single woman and yet you have children? she asked. "You have a husband? What does this mean?"

Mrs. Chase went on to describe the woman's four or five children. She also told of a violent parting the woman had with her husband.

The boarder did not comment. She rose from the chair very agitated and left. The next evening the woman returned.

"Mrs. Chase, I could not sleep until I had told you that all you said last night was true," the woman said. She gave

Mrs. Chase her real name and related all the details of the reason she had for leaving her husband.

A woman came to Mrs. Chase in 1850 suffering from what physicians believed to be the last stages of consumption (tuberculosis). Her lungs were so weak she could hardly speak. The woman's family was obliged to keep cloths wet in camphor around her mouth so she could breathe.

Mrs. Chase examined her and found the disease was not merely confined to her lungs, although they were badly affected. She gave the woman her syrup, "The Female Friend", in addition to some "Asthmatic Powders."

In a few weeks the woman began to find some relief. She returned several times to Mrs. Chase for additional medicine. About four years later the woman was cured and was able to resume her family work.

That same year H. Powers of Morrisville came to see Mrs. Chase. One of his limbs was paralyzed. He had been to see some of the best physicians in the state and none were able to help him. Mrs. Chase believed Power's trouble was brought on by a kidney infection. She ordered a six-inch plaster placed on his back and gave him some of her "Diuretic Syrup" and "P. Child's Oriental pills". She also ordered hot clothes laid on his back and limb until the disease started to lessen, and ordered liniment rubbed on his back several times each day.

Within two months Powers was able to walk without a crutch and within six months he was completely cured.

A child in Morrisville took some "corrosive sublimate" believing it be be camphor. His family, believing the child dying, called Mrs. Chase. She gave him some 'Preparation of Lobelia" which caused the boy to vomit. However, the poison had damaged the passage to his stomach. Mrs. Chase gave him tea made of "Lilly Syrup". Within a few days the youngster was in excellent condition, was able to return "to work at the mill."

Mrs. Chase made many other miraculous cures and became known as "Doctor".

When she died at the age of 67 on March 12, 1869, the local newspaper carried a long story on her remarkable career. The funeral was held in Eaton, Sunday, the 14th.

The Cazenovia Republican said in part: "Though she did not attain to a world wide celebrity in her profession, and in the several channels in which she labored for the general good, yet she was widely known, and as widely loved and appreciated.

BUFFALO TAMER

The big moment in Captain Julius H. Waterman's life occurred in the 1950's when he appeared with his buffalo, Ned and Ted on Arthur Godfrey's television program. At that time Godfrey had a weekly variety show on CBS, usually centered on some theme. The theme was "Wild West" when Captain Waterman appeared. Each of his huge bison, or buffalo weighed 1,800 pounds. Waterman managed to get one of them to kiss Godfrey.

Although he was a farmer, Captain Waterman had show blood in his veins. He had started by raising oxen on his farm near Deansboro. In the 1930's during the Madison County Fair at Brookfield, he could be seen with two huge oxen near the entrance gate and a sign, "Guess how much these oxen weigh?" There was no prize even if anyone did guess the oxen's weight correctly.

Waterman's Ox Farm had been famous throughout the eastern United States since 1822 when the Captain's grandfather, Artimus Waterman, made ox carts for his neighbors. The Captain carried on the family tradition of making ox carts and training oxen for many years. He exhibited his oxen and carts at centennial observances throughout the central and eastern sections of the United States. These included Marietta, Ohio and the 150 th anniversaries of Binghamton, the battle of Bemis Heights, near Saratoga and at Cherry Valley.

Long after he disposed of his oxen, Waterman always spoke fondly of them.

"I guess I will always remember when I was a boy, riding to church in an old ox cart with my father, uncle and aunt," he said. "For many years after I grew up I did all my farm work with them."

Waterman admitted he always liked appearing before the public as much as he enjoyed the ways of his forefathers and pioneers. For some years he had thought about owning and training a pair of buffalo. He contacted a ranger in South Dakota in 1934, who promised to secure a pair of calves for him. The ranger failed to keep his promise when the mother of one of the calves wrecked his truck. Undaunted, Waterman contacted Canadian government officials. He was granted permission to buy two calves at a cost of $50 each.

In 1939 Waterman and his sons, Harold and Earl, went to northern Canada. With the help of two Canadian rangers, two calves were finally captured. They were about eight months old and weighed 300 pounds each. The round trip from Deansboro to Canada and return with the calves covered 5,000 miles.

Waterman had a difficult time taming and training the buffalo. During the next few summers he gave open air shows at his Deansboro farm. In 1942 he exhibited them at the Madison County Fair for the first time.

The following year Waterman and his buffalo appeared with the James M. Cole Circus for 24 weeks, traveling through six states. In 1946 he became the "Buffalo Bill" of "Buffalo Bill's Wild West Show which toured the state of Maine.

"I played the great scout, all dressed up in fringed buckskins, he recalled. "The only trouble I had with the part was I couldn't shoot as well."

During that year Waterman was engaged to take his buffalo to Hollywood to appear in a Gene Autry western movie.

"It seems there was to be a scene in the picture where Autry was supposed to walk up to the buffalo and put his hands on the animal," Waterman recalled. "My buffalos were the only ones in the world that will let anyone touch them. Any other buffalo would have knocked Autry for a loop."

The Hollywood trip did not materialize. As Waterman and an Indian friend, Arnold Fryk, better known as Chief Silver Creek, were about to start their journey, the Captain became ill and went into the Veterans' Hospital at Bath.

When Waterman recuperated from his illness, he and Fryk started for Hollywood. On their way they decided to go to Brownsville, Texas. They traveled more than 7,000 miles putting on exhibitions in the Lone Star State. The tour carried them across Oklahoma, Kansas and Missouri. Waterman said he met many old timers who remembered when millions of buffalo roamed the plains.

Although he was in his 70's while traveling and showing his buffalo, Waterman had the spirit of youth. He actually was a veteran of the Spanish-American War. The title of "captain" was assumed after he obtained his buffalo.

"I enlisted as a private and went to war on May 2, 1898," he said frankly. "After training at Camp Black on Long Island

I was transferred to the Eighth Army Corps in the west. From San Francisco, our troop was shipped out on the steamer, Alemeda to the Sandwich Islands where the natives were reported about to revolt. I became a trumpeter in the corps before I was discharged from service in February, 1899," he added.

Between tours and his final days, Captain and Mrs. Waterman resided with their son and daughter-in-law, Mr. and Mrs. Harold Waterman on Route 20, between Madison and Sangerfield Center. During the summer he would have his buffalo on exhibition in front of the home. Bus loads of school children and travelers from all over the country and many foreign countries stopped to view the huge beasts and to talk with their owner.

He used to say he was thinking seriously of taking Gene Autry's advice and hitch his buffalo to a large cart and cross the continent to Hollywood.

It was a trip and dream he never was to live to see come true.

CAROLINE'S PLAYMATES

Through the open windows of her kitchen, Mrs. Carleton Rice could hear her small daughter, laughing and talking with her playmates. Mrs. Rice called to her daughter. Receiving no answer, she called again.

Irritated, Mrs. Rice went to the back door. Caroline was dancing about the yard, her hands outstretched as clinging to other hands. The mother said she thought her daughter had playmates with her. Caroline said she did have and named them.

Mrs. Rice was shocked. Caroline was alone! The invisible children were very real to the little girl, as much as dolls are to many girls and teddy bears to some children.

Caroline had three younger sisters whom she loved, but they were unable to give her the companionship she enjoyed with her invisible friends. As she grew older during those years of the 1850's, her fixation became more pronounced. If Caroline was made to stand in the corner or go to bed, her friends would always be with her.

In desperation Mrs. Rice pleaded with her husband to break the child of her "notions."

The Rice family resided on a farm on the Lake Moraine Road near Hamilton. There was nothing unusual in either parent's ancestry. Carleton Rice's parents died when he was young. He was brought up by an uncle, Dr. Pratt of Madison. Rice was well educated and well versed in local history. He often wrote scholarly articles for area newspapers. He married Miss Rhoda Klinck of Peterboro in 1845. She was a soloist in Gerrit Smith's church.

Caroline was the couple's first child, a hypersensitive girl. The thrashings she received from her father failed to drive her invisible playmates from her.

The parents consulted the family physician. He carefully examined Caroline and said she required a poultice. When this failed to bring results, he purged and bled the child. The physician even applied leeches to the girl's body to draw the "poison" from her system. When these methods failed, the doctor gave up the case. Caroline was beyond all human aid, he said.

"The rest is up to the good Lord," he pronounced solemnly. "I suggest you appeal to the Baptist minister and parishioners to pray for your child's unfortunate soul."

Stories about the Rice girl and her invisible playmates spread rapidly through Hamilton. Special prayers were said for Caroline's soul in the churches. They had as little curative affect as the threshings and bleedings she had received.

The harrassed Baptist minister met Mr. Rice as he was crossing the little bridge at the eastern end of Payne Street. He sadly told the father there was undeniable evidence that Caroline was possessed by the devil and all prayers were in vain.

Residents of the village, who had regarded the girl as "tetched" and a curiosity, began to fear her. If a housewife's bread failed to rise, it was the girl's fault or if a horse went lame, it was blamed on Caroline.

Mr. and Mr. Rice had to take their daughter out of the district school as no one would sit with her or her sisters. Rumors quickly spread, one of them that Caroline could not have her picture taken. A daguerreotype had been taken, the gossips related. When it was developed, it showed the likeness of a hideous old man, who might be the devil, instead that of the girl.

Somehow, the years passed and Caroline Rice grew into lovely young womanhood. She eventually met a physician, who loved her and did not seem to mind her invisible friends. They married and moved to California far from the scene of her tragic childhood to live "happily ever after."

THE CHRISTMAS DAY MURDERS

A mantle of snow hung heavily over the Sauquoit Valley on Christmas Day in 1835. There was no hint of the holiday in Augustus Babcock's weatherbeaten frame house on the Stone Road, a mile south of Holman City. No holly or mistletoe decorated the windows and there was no popcorn decorated tree in the parlor. Although four persons resided in the house there were no presents to exchange.

The Babcock home was full of hate. It lay so thick, it could almost be smelled when anyone entered the house. Edward Varndell, who was an Englishman and thirty years of age hated his pretty wife, Sally who was twenty five and attractive to other men. He also hated and resented Augustus Babcock, who was twenty three, the owner of the home, who allowed the Varndells to reside there. In turn, Babcock hated Varndell for his laziness, but tolerated him because of his wife. The only one no one paid any attention to was Annie, the seventeen-year old girl, who had been taken from an orphan asylum to earn her keep as a drudge. Annie hated everyone in the house. She was tired of being slapped and kicked when she did not hurry. She hated being treated like a beast of burden.

Varndell would arouse himself from his fits of brooding occasionally to accuse his wife of being intimate with his landlord. There was no reason for his suspicions. He resented the little acts of kindness Babcock showed Sally. If Babcock returned home from the village, related a humorous story he had heard in the store or stage tavern, he took his wife's laughter for a flirtation.

The neighbors no longer visited the Babcock home. Varndell practically accused his wife of infidelity in front of them.

The snow was still falling at sundown. Much to Babcock's surprise, Varndell said he would look after the cow and horses and see they were bedded down and fed. Mrs. Varndell retired to the room she shared with her husband and Annie. Babcock went to his bedroom off the kitchen.

The two women were asleep when Varndell returned from the barn. He hung his coat and hat on a peg near the stove, pulled off his leather boots and went into his bedroom. After he undressed, he crawled beneath the quilts beside his wife. Varndell was restless and unable to sleep.

Shortly before dawn he arose and slipped into the kitchen. He picked up the ax from the woodbox and quietly entered Babcock's bedroom. The young man was snoring loudly. Varndell lifted the ax and brought it down with all his strength. Again and again he struck at Babcock. When he saw his landlord was dead, he slowly made his way back to his own room. He lighted the candle and placed it on the commode near his wife. Sally was sleeping peacefully. Varndell raised the ax and brought it down on his wife. Again and again the weapon rose and fell.

Varndell never cast a glance at the cot on which Annie lay in heavy slumber. There was an avenue of escape open. Babcock's best horse was saddled and bridled in the barn, ready to carry him beyond the law. He pulled on his boots, put on his coat and hat and opened the door.

The gray mists of the morning were carrying away the night. The drifted snow was nearly to the top of the sill. Varndell pushed his way through the deep snow into the yard. Six feet of snow lay over the road and fields and was at the peak of the barn. There was no way of escape. Varndell's imagination pictured neighbors finding the bodies of Babcock and his wife, Sally. He would be caught and hanged.

In terror, he returned to the house. In one of the rooms he found a razor. As if intoxicated he staggered into his bedroom where his wife's body lay. He opened the razor and without hesitation slashed savagely at his throat. His hat tumbled from his head and his body fell across the bed.

Annie awoke about seven o'clock that Sunday morning, preparing to receive a scolding for not arising earlier. Her eyes focused on the bodies of Varndell and his wife and the blood splattered bed and floor. She found Sally still alive although her face was unrecognizable. There was nothing she could do. Slipping on her dress and shoes, Annie went to Babcock's room crying for help. He was dead.

With almost superhuman strength, Annie crawled from the house through the deep snow to reach the nearest neighbor to tell of the tragedy. The deep snow prevented Amasa S. Newberry of Sangerfield, one of Oneida County's coroners from visiting the Babcock home until two days later. A few days later Newberry impaneled a jury and took testimony from Annie and neighbors. The jury's opinion was Mrs. Varndell was innocent of any improprieties and her husband's senseless jealousy had caused the tragedy. The panel issued their verdict, "Mrs. Varndell and Mr. Babcock were willfully murdered by Edward Varndell, who subsequently committed suicide."

Annie, the drudge, may have found a better life. In death, Varndell proved more useful than in life. Denied burial, his skeleton eventually graced a closet of a Sauquoit Valley physician and was used in the study of anatomy.

THE WOMAN WITH THE WAXED HANDS

Of all the people who have tramped the roads in Smith's Valley and other sections of Madison County, no one was more picturesque than the little old woman with the "waxed hands."

She walked along the River Road between the hamlets of Eaton and Randallsville and the Eaton-Morrisville Road about 1906-1907. Because of her affliction, many kind-hearted residents along the roads gave her food and shelter.

W. Ross Clark, who resides on a part of the River Road, now known as the Cary Road, said he believed the woman's name was Mrs. Warren. Mrs. Clark, the former Marion Hall, who was born in the famous old Hatch-Hall homestead, on the road, remembered seeing the old woman about the winter of 1907 when she called at the home of her parents, Mr. and Mrs. Thomas L. Hall.

"She came to our home very early one morning and asked if she could come in and get warm," Mrs. Clark said. "Mother invited her in. The woman's feet were covered with snow. Mother, who had just finished sweeping, still had the broom in her hands. She started to brush the snow from the woman's feet. The lady stepped back and begged mother to be careful not to hurt her corns."

Mrs. Clark said according to the stories she has heard, the woman was from the Utica area and was sent out by her two brothers to beg, for her own and their support.

"She would hold out a pair of hideous looking arms and hands, all waxed and out of shape, and complain that there was no one to look out for her and she was unable to work," Mrs. Clark recalled. "She wore a shawl about her shoulders and under it was another shawl on which were pinned little bags of money given her by various persons.

Mr. Clark said when the woman came to their home she spent most of the day, wrapped in her shawl, with her feet in the stove oven.

"Father (Thomas L. Hall) was going to Eaton in the late afternoon," Mrs. Clark said, "and to get her out of the house invited her to ride up to the Madison County Home where he said they would take good care of her. S. Allen

Curtis was head of the County Home at that time. The woman told father she wasn't able to get in and out of the vehicle, so so she declined his invitation.

Later, she started out walking."

Mrs. Clark said she learned the woman also stopped at the Shapley home north of the Hall home and at the Mott Thompson residence to the south.

"The morning she left the Shapley home, Mrs. Shapley was planning to make an early start to visit relatives some distance away. She was in such a hurry she didn't take the old lady's hair down to comb it, but just slicked it back and replaced her hair combs," Mrs. Clark said.

"The morning the old woman left the Thompson home, Mrs. Thompson, who was a very sweet, kind, little old lady, took her hair down and combed it up very nicely. The woman complained and said Mrs. Shapley didn't hurt her and pull her hair the way Mrs. Thompson did."

Mrs. Clark also remembered the woman stayed at various homes in their vicinity many times.

"I presume she stopped for a day or night at every home where the occupants would take her in. News didn't get around as rapidly then and one neighbor at a distance wouldn't know what had happened at another's home for several days, especially during the winter."

Mrs. Clark said she never learned if the woman showed her false wax hands and arms while keeping her own hidden beneath her clothing.

"It was reported at one place where she stayed for the night, she heard the family talking about taking her to the County Home. After everyone had gone to bed and the house was locked for the night, she left through the second story window. The family found a pair of artificial wax arms on the bureau the next morning."

Bert Green, who resided in the large brick homestead on the Morrisville-Eaton Road, just north of Eaton, once discussed the woman with the waxed hands with Mr. and Mrs. Hall during a meeting of the old Eaton Grange in 1907.

"If I ever see her again," Green said, "I am going to take hold of those hands and find out whether they are wax or not."

Mrs. Clark said sometime after the Grange meeting she saw an article in a Utica newspaper about a woman being sent out by her brothers, equipped with a pair of waxed arms and hands, to prey on the sympathies of the country people.

Green never had a chance to discover if the woman's hands were wax or not. She failed to visit the homes along the roads any more.

ALIAS ELI PERKINS

Eli Perkins is a forgotten name today. In the late 1800's and early 1900's he ranked with the foremost humorists of the day — Mark Twain, John Billings, Artemus Ward, Uncle Remus, Eugene Field, Bill Nye and George W. Peck. Like another later humorist, named Will Rogers, Eli Perkins made humor from the topics of the day.

The Utica Saturday Globe, a famous weekly paper, in an article of October 11, 1919, classed Perkins among "The Funniest Men That Ever Lived."

"Eli Perkins" was the assumed name of the distinguished Melville Delancy Landon of the hamlet of Eaton, Madison County. Two homes Landon owned in Eaton are still standing in a good state of preservation. His grave, with its raised Coptic cross monument, is in the Eaton Rural Cemetery.

Landon was born in the hamlet, September 7, 1839. His father, John Landon came to the area from Litchfield, Conn. Landon attended the district school and Madison University (now Colgate) in Hamilton. He graduated from Union College in Schenectady in 1861.

During the Civil War he entered the service in the Clay Battalion in April, 1861, in Washington, D. C. He served in the United States Treasury. After the war, he embarked on the career of a planter in Louisana. He visited Europe in 1867 and while in Russia, he was named as secretary of the Legation in St. Petersburg.

Landon was always known for his sharp wit and humorous jottings. Under the name of Eli Perkins, he began building a reputation as a humorist with correspondence he sent to the New York Commercial Advertiser. Upon returning to the United States from Europe he embarked on a career of a professional humorist.

Landon began traveling extensively, lecturing as he went. He wrote several books, among them, "History of the Franco-Prussian War", "Saratoga in 1901", "Wit, Humor and Pathos", "Wit and Humor of the Age", "Kings of Platform and Pulpit", "Thirty Years of Wit" and "Eli Perkins on Money — Gold, Silver or Bi-metallism."

"In a book, "Library of Wit and Humor", which he edited, he asks a question in the introductory chapter, "What is wit and humor?" In his answer, Landon said "This is a question often asked, but it has never been truly answered.

"Humor is always the absolute truth, while wit is always an exaggeration. Humor occurs, while wit is pure fancy or imagination of the writer. Wit and humor are often used as synonymous, but they are really at antipodes. Humorous writings are absolutely true descriptions of scenes and incidents really occurring, while witty writings are purely fanciful descriptions of scenes and incidents which only occur in the mind of the writer."

In the Utica Saturday Globe story, Rollin Lynde Hartt, the writer, said "Melville D. Landon, who was well known to the police as Eli Perkins, set out to be a lawyer.

". . . . when it came time to make his first appearance in court, he let loose a wealth of choice rhetoric and passionate oratory," Hartt wrote, "quoting Kent and Blackstone and Littleton, citing 'precedent after precedent from the Digest of State Reports,' and as he tells us, 'winding up with a tremendous argument amid the applause of all the younger members of the bar.'

"Convinced that he had walloped the very dickens out of all imaginable opposition, he stood and waited the judge's decision, which soon came. Looking Eli squarely in the face, his Honor said, 'Your argument is good, Mr. Perkins, very good indeed, and I have been deeply interested in it. When a case comes up that your argument fits, I shall give your remarks all the consideration they deserve. Sit down!'

"This," says Eli, "is why I gave up the law and resorted to lecturing and writing for the newspapers."

Hartt said as a lecturer, Eli enjoyed a good deal the position Richard Harding Davis enjoyed as a writer — "the position that is, of a much persecuted and therefore much advertised goat. Wherever Eli bobbed up, the press took a crack at him, sometimes good naturedly, sometimes not.

"Gregory, a witling maintained by the Buffalo Express, wrote, anent one, Robert Smith, who had burnt a neighbor's house the night of Eli's lecture, 'If Mr. Smith can prove by competent witnesses that he actually did commit the great crime after hearing Eli Perkins, the jury will, no doubt, bring in a verdict of justifiable incendiarism.' "

Hartt also wrote, "Another time, Eli aired favorable opinions of the Pennsylvania gas wells, and the Chicago Times remarked that this was 'very generous on the part of Eli,' as 'Those gas wells were the only real rivals he had.' "

Melville Landon was the forerunner of today's stand-up comedian. In his character of Eli Perkins he seemed to have his favorite stories for colleges, universities and institutions. During a tour in 1897-98, he might tell about going through Chicago the previous night.

"I saw a grand procession in honor of Gambrinus," Eli said. "Such beautiful chariots, such decorated carriages and such a procession of men marching to music!

"Who rode in the chariots?" you ask.

"Why the rich millionaire beer producers and their daughters in satins and diamonds."

"Who rode in the decorated carriages?"

"The rich, wholesale dealers and their wives — the men who handle the product of the producers."

"Who rode in the one-horse carriages?"

"The prosperous saloon keepers who sell the product to the people."

"Who were the poor, sad-faced, ragged men who footed it along in the mud?"

"Oh, they were the consumers."

One of Eli Perkins' stories that always gained a laugh during his 1902 tour, went like this:

"Stephen Girard's will prevents clergymen from ever entering Girard College. One day the venerable Horace Greeley, who always wore a white tie and looked like a clergyman, was passing in.

"Here," said the Janitor, placing his arm across the doorway, "you can't pass in here as clergymen are forbidden.

"The hell they are," exclaimed the excited editor.

"Beg pardon," said the Janitor, "I made a mistake. Pass right in."

In a brochure for 1897-98, Landon had two favorite topics for lectures, "The Philosophy of Wit and Humor" and "Fun and Fact in Japan and China."

In 1901-02, he had added a third, "Stories Round the Stove."

151

Harrison Downs, who was Landon's secretary, kept track of the bookings. He was quoted in an advertisement that Perkins "can always give a date in any state from two to eight weeks after the application to speak is received."

Landon died in 1910 and with him Eli Perkins, who entertained and kept the people laughing from coast to coast.

TEKAKWITHA — LILY OF THE MOHAWKS

In the historic Mohawk Valley a bubbling hillside spring near Fonda and a statue in the Shrine of Our Lady of Martyrs at Auriesville, commemorates the memory of the saintly Kateri Tekawitha, the most famous convert of the Mohawk Indian Nation.

During the early 17th century, Ossereunon, the lowest of the three Mohawk castles occupied the site of the famous Auriesville Shrine. Situated about twelve leagues from the Dutch Fort Orange, Ossereunon was a palisaded stockade enclosing some sixty or seventy long houses. It was here Father Isaac Jogues and Rene Goupil came to convert and eventually to die martyr's deaths. On this ground hollowed by the blood of Jogues and Goupil, Tekakwitha was born in 1656, the daughter of a chief and his Christian Algonquin squaw.

Tekakwitha was one year old when Lemoyne, the name-sake of Father Jogues visited the Mohawk castles for the third time. He was held prisoner until May, 1658 when he was released and allowed to depart for New France.

During the winter of 1659-1660, smallpox scourged the village of Ossereunon, wiping out all its inhabitants. During the epidemic, Tekakwitha's parents and a brother died within a few days. Orphaned, the girl went to reside in the house of her uncle, also a chieftain. When the epidemic ended, the village was moved from the east side of Auries Creek to a new location, called Gandawagne, on the west.

While still very young, Tekakwitha learned of the inhuman cruelty of her people and their fierce hatred of the French. She saw captives tortured and burned alive. While the women and children stood in the shadows of their lodges watching the warriors rousing themselves to a state of frenzy on the fire water sold them by the Dutch traders, Tekakwitha would retire to her uncle's lodge to meditate.

The girl heard of how the French Governor Courcelle started with an expedition of 300 men to destroy the Mohawk castles and took a wrong trail. The governor returned to New France harassed by the Mohawks who killed the stragglers and took prisoners. Later the French were further incensed by the killing of a party of their officers by a chief named Agariata, near Lake Champlain. Chasy, a nephew of the Marquis DeTracy, was among those killed. Another nephew, Leroles, was taken a prisoner. The Mohawks returned the prisoners and asked for peace. DeTracy ended the negotiations by hanging Agariata.

With a force of 1,300 fighting men, including Canadians, regulars, "blue coats" and Indian scouts, DeTracy advanced into the Mohawk country to wipe out the fierce warriors.

As the army approached their strongholds, the Mohawks abandoned Ossereunon and the next castle, Anageren, concentrating all their fighting strength at the chief upper castle, Tionontogen. Tekakwitha, with the other women and children, was forced to hide in the woods while the warriors prepared to fight the French army.

Advancing on the two lower castles, DeTracy found them and several other small villages deserted. After putting them to the torch, the Marquis decided to return to Canada, thinking he had conquered the Mohawk country. An Alqonquin squaw, who had once been a Mohawk captive, informed DeTracy of the third and larger castle farther above. It was approaching dusk and the French soldiers were weary from marching through swamps and forests. They were given the order to advance. Clutching a gun the Algonquin squaw led the way toward the upper castle.

While waiting the attack, the Mohawks had several captives brought into the public square and tortured to appease their war-god, Aireskei. The torture had just begun when the bugles of DeTracy's army were heard. Tekakwitha could see the largest army ever to enter the Mohawk Valley as the French rounded the base of the cliff of the Little Nose and came along the south shore of the river.

File after file, the French came with drums beating and banners flying in the early evening breeze. The Mohawks crouched behind their wooden ramparts on the hill. As the French deployed for the attack, the Mohawks, led by their chief, opened the hill gate and fled in panic up the steep incline to join their squaws and children in the safety of the forest.

DeTracy was surprised to find the castle deserted. He ordered the cornfields and the castle and its lodges burned. When the French left the valley, the Mohawks began to rebuild their castle. It was too late in the season to plant corn and vegetables. The warriors were able to kill enough game during the winter to keep their people from starving. By the spring of 1667, the Mohawks were a miserable people, but at peace with their French and Algonquin enemies. New terms of peace between the French and Mohawks were concluded that summer in Quebec. In July, the Mohawk deputies left the city accompanied by three Jesuit priests, Fathers Fromin, Pierron and Bruyas. They were to remain with the Mohawks, not only to erect chapels and convert, but as a visible sign of peace and the power of the church and New France. A Mohawk scouting party guided the party from Lake George to the Mohawk River, probably at Dadaniscara, where they crossed to the ruined Ossereunon. The previous year Fathers Jogues and Goupil had been greeted with cruelty by the Mohawks. At this time, the three Jesuits were received as ambassadors of a victorious foe. Most of the warriors were absent from Ossereunon, having gathered at their partly rebuilt capital at Tionnontogen for a drunken festival.

The Jesuits were lodged in the home of Tekakwitha's uncle. The girl served them food while her family was absent. She was touched by the kindness of the priests and their regularity of prayer. It was probably this, more than anything else, that led to Tekakwitha's conversion to Christianity.

A great public reception was held by the three Jesuits in the public square of Tionnontegen, the Mohawk capital. Father Fremin previously erected a pole some forty or fifty feet in height. At the top a wampum belt was suspended. He then told the assembled Mohawks the governor would hang the first warriors who killed a Frenchman or any of their allies.

The Mohawks regarded the pole symbol with awe. Hanging was more dreaded than death by fire. Greatly impressed, the Mohawks gave up a Frenchman who they held as captive and promised to release twelve Algonquins. They also promised to help the Jesuits erect a log chapel.

Efforts to christianize the Mohawks proved futile.

Eventually Father Pierron replaced Father Fremin, who was sent west to the Oneida Nation. Father Pierron located his mission, called St. Peter's, at the castle of Caughnawaga.

After the fear of the French diminished, the Mohawks frequently treated the priests cruelly and often threatened their lives. In a few months Father Boniface arrived at Tionontegen to aid Father Pierron in his labor. Father Jean de

Lamberville arrived in 1673 to relieve Father Boniface, whose health was broken by the rigors of life on the frontier.

Father de Lamperville stopped at the home of Tekakwitha's uncle. Here he met the girl who announced her intention of being baptised and confirmed.

Tekakwitha, at seventeen, had grown into a tall, beautiful girl. Her long black hair was well-oiled, parted in the middle of her head and descending in a long plait down her back. She was wearing a chemise of deer skin, met at the waist by a well-trimmed petticoat reaching to her knees. Under this, long richly embroidered leggings covered her legs to the moccasins. A necklace of beads hung around her throat while a crimson blanket hanging from her shoulders, enveloped her form.

Her life had been none too happy. Since her adopted sister, Anastasia Tegenhatsihongo had married and became converted, Tekakwitha's relatives urged her to marry. Many braves had lain offerings at her feet, all which she ignored.

As soon as Tekakwitha announced her intention of becoming converted, her uncle treated her more cruelly than before. Despite this, Tekakwitha made ready for her baptism on Easter Sunday, 1676.

The log chapel was richly decorated for the ceremony. The Christian converts, who loved the girl, adorned the interior with beaver and elk skins. There were bear skin rugs and buffalo skins from the far western country on the floor. Belts of wampum hung from the rafters. The altar was decorated with blossoming shrubs and clusters of wild flowers.

As Tekakwitha and her two attendants approached the doorway, Father de Lamberville's choir of small Indian children began to sing softly. The Jesuit, in surplice and violet stole, advanced to meet Tekakwitha and accompany her to the altar.

"Katherine," he asked clearly so all could hear, "what dost thou ask of the Church of God?"

"Faith," the girl replied softly.

"What doth faith lead to?"

"Life everlasting," she answered.

"If then, thou will enter into life," Father de Lamberville continued, "keep the commandments. Thou shalt love the Lord, thy God, with all thy soul and with all thy mind and thy neighbor as thyself."

The words and signs deeply impressed the girl. Breathing on her three times as she knelt with bowed head, the Jesuit exorcised the Evil on, saying, "Go out of her, thou unclean spirit. Give place to the Holy Spirit, the Parachlete!"

Then raising Tekakwitha's head, Father de Lamberville signed her forehead and breast with the cross.

After her conversion, the woman of her uncle's household left her in peace. Then gradually they began their former tirade. Her uncle bore Father Boniface a grudge for converting another chief named Kryn. Kryn led many of his followers to New France, weakening the strength of the Mohawk village. The uncle tried to intimidate his niece by sending a drunken warrior to frighten her. The warrior entered the cabin and rushed at her with a raised tomahawk. The girl bowed her head and waited for the blow. It was never struck. Seeing the girl could not be frightened, the warrior felt ashamed and left.

Tekakwitha's aunt plotted against her, striving to undermine her faith. She went to Father de Lamberville concerning her niece's morals. When the Jesuit learned of this falsity, he severely reprimanded the old woman.

Tekakwitha joined the Mohawks in their spring hunt in 1677 into the region now known as Saratoga. When she returned to Caughnawaga, her adopted sister's husband visited her, bringing an Oneida chief named Garonhiague, who was a leading convert among the Iroquois in New France.

Tekakwitha's uncle was not at home, as he was on one of his periodic visits to Albany. Garonhiague and her brother-in-law pursuaded the girl to escape the tyranny of her uncle's household. Tekakwitha agreed. The three entered a canoe and started down the Mohawk toward present Amsterdam. It was here they found the trail to Lake George.

As soon as he returned from Albany, the uncle learned of his niece's flight. He seized his gun and shook it in rage before starting in pursuit, swearing to kill all three. The uncle eventually overtook the three. Hearing his approach, Tekakwitha and the two braves secreted themselves in the underbrush. The old chief passed by without finding them. At length he gave up the chase and returned to the castle.

After a long canoe voyage across Lake George and Lake Champlain, Tekakwitha and her companions reached Caughnawaga on the St. Lawrence River. Tekakwitha was welcomed by her adopted sister.

In her new home the maiden became known as Kateri, the Iroquois corruption of Katherine, her baptismal name. She became the outstanding convert at the Misson of St. Xavier de Sault. The converted Indians often practiced severe penances, despite the fact their past sins had been washed away by baptism. Some beat themselves with switches until the blood flowed. Others dragged logs of wood all day with an iron belt about their bodies.

Kateri had a precise version of the love for sacrifical suffering. To give the Lady some proof of her affection on the Feast of Purification, she went barefoot through the snow, while reciting her rosary several times. At other times she wore a crown of spikes on her head. She had her friends beat her with sticks and upon learning the greatest suffering was caused by fire she branded herself with blazing fagots.

During the winter of 1680, Kateri's strength began to fail and she forsaw approaching death. It was necessary to take her to church on a sled. She finally became so feeble, she could barely move and remained alone in her cabin. Father Cholonec recorded that Tekakwitha's sufferings became intense during the last two months of her life. She remained peaceful and content, and remarked she was "happy to die on the cross." She was only twenty four when she died on Holy Wednesday, April 17, 1680.

Kateri had been only dead a quarter of an hour when a change began taking place in her body. The saintly girl's face had been pitted with smallpox from the age of four. Her mortifications during her final years had greatly disfigured her. Suddenly all the scars vanished and she became beautiful.

Later, commenting on this miracle, Father Cholonec said, "I speak frankly when I say that the first thought that came to me was that Kateri had entered at that moment into celestial glory."

Her remains were interred with solemn ceremony at Caughnawaga and a large wooden cross was raised to mark her resting place. In 1880 a large granite monument was sent from the Mohawk Valley to replace the wooden cross. It bore the following inscription:

"Kateri Tekakwitha
April 17, 1680
Onkew Onwe — Katsitsiio Teiotsitsianekaron
'The fairest flower that ever bloomed among the Red Men.)"

HARRISON FRANK

One early night in July, 1862, Harrison Frank of Wampsville received a premonition of disaster. Try as he might he was unable to shake off the feeling that swept over him.

Frank had long been prominent in Masonic circles. He was the second master of Canastota Lodge No. 231. As a representative of the Grand Lodge in Central New York, he traveled with the Right Worshipful William H. Drew, the grand lecturer, visiting other lodges.

A few days before starting on the round of official visits, Frank enlisted in the new 157th Regiment. New York Volunteers, as a second lieutenant, in Company G.

The night before he departed with his regiment, he attended his last meeting of the Masonic Lodge in Canastota. Acting as senior deacon, Frank was invited by the master to take his seat in the East. As the master started to pound his gavel to bring the meeting to order, the wooden head flew off the gavel and struck Frank in the breast.

Harrison Frank stood motionless, his face suddenly pale in the lamplight. The masons quieted suddenly.

"I'll not return here again," Frank said in a choked voice. "I think that gavel foretells I'm to die."

The lodge brothers gathered around and tried to lessen his fears, but a curtain of tragedy hung over the meeting.

On July 2, 1863, Captain Frank fell on the bloody battlefield at Gettysburg with a bullet in his breast, at the exact spot where the head of the gavel had struck the previous year.

Captain Frank was the first enlisted officer from Madison County to die in battle.

www.ingramcontent.com/pod-product-compliance
Lightning Source LLC
Chambersburg PA
CBHW020010140726
47904CB00018B/2213